P9-APH-706

JAMES STEVENSON

The Unprotected Witness

GREENWILLOW BOOKS, New York

Greenwillow Books, a division of William Morrow & Company, Inc.,
1350 Avenue of the Americas, New York, NY 10019.
Printed in the United States of America
First Edition
10 9 8 7 6 5 4 3 2 1

Library of Congress Cataloging-in-Publication Data
Stevenson, James, (date)
The unprotected witness / by James Stevenson.
p. cm.
Sequel to: The bones in the cliff.
Summary: After the murder of his father, who has been hiding under the Witness Protection Program, Pete finds himself the target of sinister men who seem to think he knows where a large sum of money is hidden.
ISBN 0-688-15133-7
[1. Witnesses—Protection—Fiction.
2. Organized crime—Fiction.
3. Murder—Fiction.
4. Buried treasure—Fiction.] I. Title.
PZ7.S84748Up 1997
[Fic]—dc21
96-39130 CIP AC

For Tom

Contents

PART II: NEW YORK

PART I

MISSOURI

CHAPTER 1

Down the Fire Escape

We took an early plane out of LaGuardia, heading for Missouri—my best friend Rootie, her grandmother Mrs. Bowditch, and me.

The United States marshals were going to meet us in St. Louis. Then we'd drive down to the Ozarks together.

It was a rainy day. We sat on the runway for a while, then we took off into the rain, and the water streamed across my window.

Mrs. Bowditch opened her bag and took out her new Roger Tory Peterson bird book. She already had a bunch of bird books, but she'd bought this one specially for the trip: *Birds of the Western States.*

Rootie asked the attendant what was for lunch. The attendant told her. "Oh, *please,*" said Rootie, and pulled her baseball cap down over her eyes. "See you in St.

Louis," she said to me, and went to sleep. Like that: bam.

I figured we were crossing the Bronx. I tried to go to sleep like Rootie, but it didn't work for me.

My father and I had lived in the Bronx one winter. I remembered the sound of planes flying low.

We were on the run, my father and I. We lived on the fifth floor of a tenement, a couple of blocks from Hunts Point Avenue. The whole time we were there, my father never once left that room.

He watched TV on an old set where everything looked like smoke. But he didn't give a damn. He was doing a quart of vodka a day.

I know, because I had to go get it. The same with food. All take-out: Chinese. Pizza. Chinese. Pizza. Chinese . . .

The stairs in the tenement had no lights. I guess they burned out, or else people took them, but there were never any lights. The steps were narrow and full of garbage. You had to walk down slowly, touching the wall, using whatever light came from under people's doors. Sometimes a person would be standing in a hall, silent, not moving. You wouldn't know he was there till you practically bumped into him.

I hated those stairs.

I got the vodka from one of the raggedy-looking guys who hung out in front of the liquor store. I got to know them. They were okay. In fact, they were the only friends I had. After a while, they'd see me coming and start arguing which of them was going to buy me the vodka. I'd hand the money to one of them, then I'd go around the corner and wait in the hall of a deserted brownstone. The floor was tile—I'd look at the patterns and the faded colors while I waited. I thought of long ago, and guys kneeling in the hall, putting each tile exactly in its place. Now half the tiles were cracked or missing, and the house was empty.

Then one of the raggedy guys would bring a paper bag with the vodka, and I'd put it in my book bag and go back up to the room.

Some days I'd take a detour past the neighborhood school. If it was morning, crowds of kids about my age would be swarming around the door, yelling and laughing. If it was noon, they'd be in the yard, shooting baskets and fooling around, shoving one another, joking, pretending to fight.

I'd stand and watch from across the street. I hadn't been to a school in over two years.

I wanted to go in that yard and do whatever those kids did. There was a girl with black hair. I liked the way she moved. I wished I could talk to her. One day I built up my courage and crossed the street and stood near the wire fence near the basketball court. A kid jumped high, turned in the air, and slam-dunked the ball. I yelled "Awwright!"

I wished I hadn't. A couple of guys glared at me, like What are you doing around here? The black-haired girl said something in Spanish to her friends, and they giggled.

After that, I never went by the school anymore.

At night I brought my father the pizza or the Chinese that we'd eat. Then I'd ask him if I could go out and walk around awhile. That time of day, you couldn't tell what my father might do. I wanted to get out of there.

"Okay," he said. "But hurry up. And keep your eyes open. If you see anybody hanging around down on the street, get up here as fast as you can."

There was a place I went to sometimes. It was an open lot where a tenement had burned out. Just a bunch of bricks lying around, and weeds.

I'd wait across the street.

Pretty soon, when it was dark except for the streetlight

down the block, the empty lot would begin to tremble and shiver. The lot came alive, jittering.

It was rats. Big rats. Hundreds of them. When they started to cross the sidewalk, I took off.

Fast.

But then I'd go back another night. It was weird. I didn't want to go, but at the same time . . . you know.

One cold night, I was coming back from the rats, and I saw a big black car pull slowly up to our building. Just easing in. Then the headlights went out. I could see cigarettes being lit. Then there was just the glow as they smoked. Two men got out. They stretched, straightened their clothes.

My heart was hammering. How could I warn my father?

I walked casually past the men toward the building. One step after the other, nice and slow.

I almost reached the door.

"Hey!" called one of the men. I jumped. "Yeah, you," he said. "Come here."

I thought: run. Maybe I could get to the door and up the stairs ahead of them. Maybe I could throw some garbage down the steps in their way. . . .

Or maybe I could just walk on down the block and

around the corner, and keep on going. I could leave my father exactly where he was, with his vodka and his Chinese food. . . .

The man stepped forward and grabbed my coat. "I said come here," he said. "What's the matter—don't you speak English?"

I made a sign with my fingers—"a little bit."

"Okay," said the man. He had a high, raspy voice. "You understand money, right?" He pulled a bill from his pocket. It was a five. He waved it in front of my face. "Answer this question. You know a man who lives in this building—an Anglo? He's a drunk." He tipped a bottle with his hand. "You seen this Anglo?"

"*Borracho?*" I said. That was what the liquor store owner yelled at the raggedy men. I tipped my hand the way he did.

"Right," said the man. "Where is this man?"

I pointed at our building and waved my hands: no, no, no. I pointed down the block and raised two fingers.

"Two doors down?" he said.

"*Si,*" I said. "Two." I smiled and reached for the five-dollar bill.

He yanked it back and put it in his pocket.

"Later," he said. "*If* you told the truth." They strolled away, heading for the other building.

I went up the stairs like a rocket and pounded on the door, yelling, "Two men—on the street—asking about you!" In a second the door was open, and my father grabbed his coat and his suitcase and said, "Come on!" He was cold sober now, and he climbed over the radiator, out the window, and onto the fire escape. I followed him, and we ran down the icy metal steps, slipping, grabbing the rail, down all four floors. At the bottom rung, my father threw the suitcase into the snow, then dropped to the snow himself, his coat flying out around him like a crow.

I was scared to drop. It was maybe ten feet. "Don't be a coward," yelled my father. "Jump!"

I wanted to say, "Catch me." But I could see he wasn't going to do that. I let go, dropped, and fell in the snow, face first. It was freezing. I felt like crying. My father yanked me out of the snow. "Come on! We're going to the subway!"

We ran down the alley. He climbed up on a garbage can and threw his suitcase over a fence. Then he went over the fence after it.

A dog started barking.

I looked back up to see if the men were following us. I was shaking all over. A man walked by slowly. He looked down the alley. But he kept going, and then he was out of sight. I swung over the fence. My father was already running down the street, holding his suitcase to his chest like a football, heading for the subway.

We stood on the subway stairs, keeping out of sight while we waited for a train. My father asked about the men. "They were cops?" he said.

"No," I said. "Unless maybe they were plainclothes."

"What did they look like?" he said.

"Just regular," I said. "One of them had a high voice, kind of screechy."

"I know him," said my father. And that was the last thing he said.

I guess it didn't matter who it was—cops or bad guys. They were both after him. What mattered was they had found him.

We rode all the way to Coney Island that night. When we finally got there, we walked a long way. Sleet was coming down. You could see the silhouette of the old roller coaster a few blocks away. We came to a crummy building.

In the entrance, my father had to light a match to read the names. Then he pushed one of the buzzers. Nothing happened. He buzzed again, and again.

Finally a tinny voice came over the intercom: "Who the hell is it?"

"It's me—Harry," said my father. "Let me in."

"Harry?" said the voice.

"Yeah, Harry," said my father. "Open up, Nick! We're freezing, my boy and me."

"What are you, crazy coming here?" said the voice. "Get the hell out before I call the cops."

"Nick—come on!" said my father.

"I'm calling the cops," said the voice. "Right now."

The intercom went off.

We went out into the street again.

"What a bastard," I said. "Who was that guy?"

"My best friend," he said.

C H A P T E R 2

The Stranger in the Coffin

When we landed in St. Louis, two United States marshals met us. I saw them first. One was tall and hefty, the other was small, with a tight jaw. The big guy was chewing gum. When he spotted us, he took the gum out of his mouth, wrapped it in a piece of paper, and stuck it in his pocket.

They told us how sorry they were about what had happened. The big guy explained the plans to Mrs. Bowditch. Rootie turned to the short marshal.

"What's it like being a United States marshal, sir?" asked Rootie. "Do you very often shoot people?"

The marshal didn't answer. He just frowned and shook his head.

"You must meet a lot of sleazeballs who rat on their buddies, don't you?" said Rootie.

The marshal glared at her.

"Do you protect big-time mobsters?"

"That's confidential," said the marshal.

"Do you pack a rod? I don't see one," said Rootie.

"You're not supposed to," said the marshal.

"It must be small," said Rootie. "What do you do with it at night? Do you wear it, or do you put it under your pillow?"

"Why don't you go buy yourself a candy bar?" said the marshal. He walked away.

"Why did you do that, Rootie?" I said.

Rootie was laughing too hard to answer. "Somebody has to do it," she said finally.

She was a tough cookie, Rootie. She loved to laugh, and she loved to take chances. I really liked Rootie.

We got into a rented car and followed the marshals down through Missouri, heading for the Ozarks. The roads were narrow and twisty.

Rootie was looking out the window, counting cows and reading billboards. "Hey, can we stop at Jesse James Cavern?" she said. "Six miles ahead. Turn right."

"This is not a sightseeing tour, Rosalie," said Mrs. Bowditch. (She only called her Rosalie when she was correcting her, or pretending to. The rest of the time it was Rootie—short for Rootie Kazootie, some tough little kid in an old newspaper comic strip.)

"I know," said Rootie. "I just thought it would be good for Pete's morale. Wouldn't you like to see Jesse James Cavern, Pete?"

"Whatever," I said.

"I do loathe that word," said Mrs. Bowditch. "No offense, dearie."

I just wanted to get the day over with. I didn't even know where we were going—just to the Ozark Mountains. Some little town where the U.S. marshals had hidden my father—"protecting" him so he could be a witness for the government and testify in a big trial.

Well, he wasn't going to testify for anybody. Not now.

"I'm starving," said Rootie. "If we come to a McDonald's, let's stop."

"Dream on," I said. "This state is deserted."

"I brought some lovely pears," said Mrs. Bowditch. "They're in my bag in the trunk."

She honked at the marshals' car and flashed her lights, and pulled over to the side of the road.

She was opening the trunk when the marshals came barreling down the road, looking all around.

"What's wrong?" shouted the tall one.

"Would you care for a delicious pear?" said Mrs. Bowditch.

The marshals said no, thank you. They sat in their car and smoked cigarettes while we ate the pears.

We started driving again.

Suddenly the car began swerving around. I sat up. Mrs. Bowditch was leaning over the steering wheel and peering up through the top of the windshield.

"What is it?" I said.

"Possible Swainson's hawk," she said. "Dig out my Roger Tory Peterson, Rootie—it's in my purse."

Rootie got the Peterson bird book and began reading aloud about different types of hawks, while Mrs. Bowditch looked this way and that way and the car zigzagged down the highway.

I must have fallen asleep because the next thing I knew we were slowing down, coming into a town square. It was a sad-looking place: boarded-up brick buildings, a movie theater that said CLOSED, a gas station with no pumps. In the middle of the square was a flagpole and a little garden, but there wasn't any flag and the garden was weeds.

We parked in front of the Davenport Funeral Home.

There were state police and cops standing around, and a small crowd of ordinary people.

The tall marshal came over and leaned in our window. "There's a photographer here. We're going to try to keep him away from you, Peter, but if you see him, just turn away or put your hand over your face."

"Why?" I said.

"Just a precaution."

"What's going on?" said Rootie.

"We don't want Peter's face in the media," said the marshal.

"That's another word I happen to loathe," said Mrs. Bowditch. "If you mean newspapers, perhaps you could just say so."

"Newspapers, TV, whatever," he said.

"What precaution?" said Rootie in a loud voice. She was getting mad.

"Please lower your voice, young lady," said the marshal.

"Don't call me young lady!" yelled Rootie.

The marshal glanced over his shoulder. Then he said, "There are individuals who believe that Peter's father was in possession of a considerable amount of money at the time of his death."

"What's wrong with that?" said Mrs. Bowditch.

"It was not his money," said the marshal.

"Oh," said Mrs. Bowditch.

"He never told *me* about any money," I said. "He didn't have any money."

We went into the funeral home. It had thick rugs, and soft music was playing, and there were sweet flowers, really stinky. I wanted to get out of there.

We shook hands with the funeral director. His hand was soft and squishy like the rugs. He was all spiffed up and you could smell his suit had just come back from the cleaners.

"Big shot," whispered Rootie. "He's got the only successful business in town."

When it was time to go into the room with the casket, I started to sweat, and I said to Rootie, "I think I'll skip this part. I'll meet you in the car."

Rootie grabbed my hand. "It'll be okay." she said. "We'll go in together."

The casket was sitting in the middle of the room with the satin top open, like a big jewelry case. I squeezed Rootie's hand tight, took a deep breath, and looked inside.

I thought that they had made a mistake—that it wasn't my father.

He was wearing a suit, a clean white shirt, and a tie. His hair was combed. He was shaved. There was no bags under his eyes and no wrinkles. His face was smooth. His mouth was set in a pleasant little smile.

"They sure fixed him up," whispered Rootie.

"Shhh," said Mrs. Bowditch.

I guess he had been shot in the back. He was okay in front.

"Perhaps you would like to spend a moment alone with your father?" said the funeral director.

"Go ahead, Pete," said Rootie. "I'll be outside."

Everybody left.

I felt like I should say something to my father—something about how I missed him and wished he was back. How I was grateful he had taken care of me all the years. Never dumped me or anything. I know I slowed him down. He could have dumped me.

But the truth was, I wasn't very grateful at all. Why did I have to live with an outlaw all my life? I hadn't done anything.

So finally I didn't say anything at all. We never used to talk much, my father and I. Why start now?

I settled for "Good-bye, Dad."

C H A P T E R 3

The Picture on the Cup

On the sidewalk outside the funeral home, a skinny old man was waiting for us. He looked like a bloodhound—red eyes and jowls hanging down. White hair stuck out over his ears. He was twisting his hat in his hands.

"I was a friend of the deceased," he said in a shaky voice. "I'm real sorry about this."

We shook hands.

"My name is Creech," he said. "I thought you might want to see where your daddy lived. Maybe there's something of his you'd like to take."

The marshals said that it would be okay, so Creech got into a battered green pickup truck and we followed him out of town, the marshals behind us. After a couple of miles, we turned down a dirt road. It went past a farm, and then we came to some woods. We parked at the side of the road, and everybody got out.

"Listen!" said Mrs. Bowditch. She watched a bird fly overhead. "Do you hear that sound?" She took out her Peterson's, flipped through it, and then read aloud: " 'Rattling or clicking notes in flight suggesting the winding of a cheap watch . . . ' Isn't that exactly what we heard?"

Rootie said, "It sounded like an expensive watch to me."

"Maybe a Rolex," I said. Mrs. Bowditch ignored us.

"Smith's Longspur," she said. "Never seen in the East."

She began explaining about birds to the marshals while Rootie threw rocks at a telephone pole.

Mr. Creech started down a path into the woods. "Your daddy and me, we were buddies," he said. He lit what was left of a burnt cigarette. I guess he'd put it out at the funeral place. "Most nights we'd have a little drink together." He coughed. "He used to tell me how he had a swell son back East. He was real proud of you, and he sure missed you. . . ." He shook his head. "Terrible thing, what's happened. . . . Your daddy wasn't the easiest man in the world to get along with. Guess you know that. He was a boozer. That's the truth. But can you blame him? He knew there was people looking for him. But we had some laughs, him and me. I remember one night—he had a snootful—he said to me, 'Can you keep a secret?'

"I says, 'Hell, yes. I don't know nobody to tell it to anyways.' We laughed over that, then he whispers, 'I got over two million dollars buried in a secret place.'

"I look at him, and I says, 'Well, ain't that a coincidence? So do I!' We laughed so hard we near fell off our chairs. We had some good times, him and me."

The others were following us down the path now. Mr. Creech didn't say anything for a while. He was glancing into the woods.

Mr. Creech took a quick look over his shoulder—Mrs. Bowditch and Rootie and the marshals were maybe twenty yards behind us—and said to me in a low voice, "Listen to me now, sonny. I got here a letter to you from your daddy. You know he wasn't allowed to write no letters. Don't look at me, don't do nothing, just keep on walking—but when I get the chance I'm going to hand it to you. Then you stick it in your pocket fast as you can."

We kept walking. The path took a turn around a tree,

and right then Mr. Creech slapped that letter into my hand, and I jammed it into my pocket.

We came to a clearing, and there was a log cabin overlooking a valley and, far away, low blue-green mountains, rolling like the ocean, one wave after another.

"Lovely view of the Ozarks," said Mrs. Bowditch, catching up.

"Don't go wandering, ma'am," said Mr. Creech. "Lots of bears around here." I glanced around. No bears in sight. Yet.

The front door of the cabin was open. The marshals went in first.

A minute later one of them came to the door. "Somebody's been in here," said the tall one. "It's a mess. Maybe you'd rather not come in."

Rootie and Mrs. Bowditch and I looked at one another. "I want to see where he lived," I said. "I don't care."

"Me, too," said Rootie.

"Very well," said Mrs. Bowditch.

We went in.

The cabin was totally trashed. Drawers yanked out and dumped, cabinets emptied, chairs and tables upside down, garbage strewn all over. A refrigerator was lying on its side, everything spilled out of it. The stovepipe had been broken off, wood thrown around, smashed plates and bottles and glasses everywhere. A plaid sofa was slashed open, and the guts pulled out. I didn't see his suitcase.

"Look," said Rootie, picking up a coffee cup. The handle was broken off. "It's got a picture of you and your father."

I took the cup. I hadn't seen it for a long time. I didn't know my father had kept it.

When I was about six years old, my father had taken me to an amusement park. I don't even know where. I think it was my birthday. I went on some kiddie rides, and my father stood watching. I wanted to go on one of the big roller coasters, but I was too little. Then I saw the Tunnel of Fear, and I begged my father to take us on that. I wanted to be tough like he was. We got into a little green boat together and went floating into a dark tunnel. You could hear the screeching up ahead. A skeleton tried to grab us, then a bat flew by and a hideous witch reached out at us, cackling. I was so scared I dived under the seat of the boat and stayed there, curled up with my hands over my ears and my eyes shut, for the whole ride.

When we finally floated out into the sunlight, I was ashamed of myself. I guess my father could tell.

We came to a souvenir booth where they take your picture. He said, "Come on." We went in. You could get a big picture in a frame, or on a T-shirt or a coffee cup.

We took the cup.

This was the cup—stained and chipped, without a handle—and there was my father's face and mine. You could see I'd been crying.

Under the picture it said in fancy letters: BEST FRIENDS.

Mrs. Bowditch said, "Shall we go now?"

"Yeah, let's get out of here," said Rootie.

"Anything you'd like to take with you, Peter?" asked the marshal.

I said, "I don't know."

They left.

I walked out onto the porch off the living room. The screen door slammed behind, like a gun. There was a rickety old chair. I looked at the mountains and thought about how many times my father had probably sat in that chair and looked at them. I bet those mountains could make a lonely person feel a lot worse.

"Come on, Pete!" called Rootie.

I took the cup and threw it as far as I could over the treetops.

CHAPTER 4

Collyer's Spring

We drove back to St. Louis the next day. The marshals weren't with us anymore—their job was over—so we took a route just north of Arkansas. There was a bird sanctuary that Mrs. Bowditch wanted to see called Collyer's Spring.

I stretched out on the backseat while Rootie and her grandmother argued. Rootie was giving her a lot of guff about how she wanted to go in the other direction to Branson, Missouri, and see all those crummy country-western acts. "We never see anything," she said.

I thought about opening my father's letter. But I knew it was just going to make me feel worse. I felt lousy enough already.

We pulled over at a park sign that said COLLYERS SPRING. Mrs. Bowditch put on her binoculars, grabbed her Roger Tory Peterson, and walked down toward the woods. "A little exercise will do you wonders, kiddies," she said. "See you in a bit."

Rootie was an information junkie, so she went over to the sign right away.

"Hey, Pete," she said. "Listen. 'Collyer's Spring produces enough water in twenty-four hours to fill the needs of New York City for one whole day. . . . No one knows where the water comes from. Divers have been sent down to try to locate the source, but it remains a mystery.' "

"You want to see it?" I said.

"Are you kidding?" said Rootie. She called to Mrs. Bowditch, "We're going to look at the spring." Her grandmother waved.

We checked the paths on the map. The spring was maybe half a mile away. We ran down a twisty path covered with yellow leaves and slippery pine needles. Every so often there'd be a mark painted on a tree trunk. "Lewis and Clark," said Rootie.

We crossed a log bridge and went uphill. In some places it was pretty steep, and you had to grab a branch to get up. We walked along a ridge for a while, and then we were going almost straight down. Stones rolled away under our feet and went bouncing down the hill.

Then we heard the noise.

A roar was coming from ahead of us. We couldn't see anything, but the sound got louder and louder. We went around a big rock cliff and saw a huge wall of stone, striped like the Grand Canyon. A river came out from under it and spun into a white whirlpool, maybe a hundred feet across. The water kept tumbling away, then racing down the valley. The noise was like a tornado.

Rootie couldn't bother to follow the path anymore. She didn't stop for a minute, just went straight down like a mountain climber, hand over hand, using crevices in the rock.

I followed her. I didn't want to, but I did. The rock was wet and slippery. Every time I stuck my hand in a crevice, I thought of rattlesnakes, coiled up in the darkness. I was pretty sure Missouri had rattlesnakes. Maybe it was even famous for them. It definitely had bears. I didn't know whether to watch for bears behind me, or rattlesnakes in front of me.

When I got to the riverbank, Rootie was sitting down, leaning against a big tree that bent over the water. We watched the spring. It was like seeing where the world began. Even though the spring was noisy and violent, throwing foam, it was peaceful, too. The air was so fresh you could almost touch it.

At our feet, a log had come to rest, bumping against the shore, making a shallow pool. We took off our sneakers and stood in the pool. The water felt great. You could see golden pebbles on the bottom. I grabbed a stick that was jammed between some rocks and threw it out into the rapids. Rootie and I watched as it dived out of sight, then came up again, and went over the rocks, and dipped, and popped up. It stuck for a minute between boulders, then lifted off and sailed away.

I thought about my father now. I wished he could be in a place like this, sitting beside a tumbling river where big trees leaned over the rapids. I wished that his terrible life and his terrible death would be washed away, and that a new life for him could start in a canyon like this, where a spring came whirling out from under a mountain.

Though I didn't know it then, Collyer's Spring would run along beside me, long after we left Missouri. At night sometimes in New York, I would hear its roar louder than the sirens of the city, and I would feel the cool air on my face. Some nights, it would carry me to sleep.

Rootie and I walked back through the woods. When

we got to the car, Mrs. Bowditch was making notes in her bird book.

"I'm almost positive I got a scissor-tailed flycatcher," she said, "and a possible Sprague's pipit."

"Score!" said Rootie.

"A day well spent!" said Mrs. Bowditch. "Did you run into Mr. Smith?"

"Who's that?" I said.

"The bird-watcher. He followed you down the trail."

I looked at Rootie. She was staring straight ahead.

"I told him he wouldn't do very well without binoculars," said Mrs. Bowditch. "But he said he was just a beginner."

"Did he come back out again?" I said.

"I didn't see him," said Mrs. Bowditch. "His car is parked over there."

We looked back. The car was gone.

CHAPTER 5

Rootie

It's funny how things work out.

The summer before on Cutlass Island, Rootie had been my best friend. I thought I was her best friend, too. Maybe I was. But it's funny how things work out.

The first time we met was one morning down in the harbor at the ferryboat landing. I was hanging around, waiting for the ferry to come in.

My father and I had moved into a bungalow in May. For a while it seemed like we were safe. Then late one night a phone call came. It was the man my father called Looney Tunes. He said he knew where we lived, and he'd be coming out to see us.

After that my father sat in a chair by the window, a glass of vodka in one hand and a gun on the table. He watched the road.

My job was to go meet every ferry that came in to the island. That was three times a day. I was supposed to watch for a big guy with a cigar, and if I saw him I'd run to the phone and call my father.

That's why I was down at the dock. Rootie was just cruising around on her bike. She liked to ride through the village in the middle of the sidewalk and scare tourists. She lived with her grandmother, Mrs. Bowditch, in a big old house not far from our bungalow. Her parents were someplace else, like the Dominican Republic, getting a divorce. Later on, I learned she practically never saw them.

Rootie knew every inch of Cutlass Island—secret paths through the woods, deserted buildings, beaches where nobody ever went, and huge cliffs. She ran straight down the cliffs. That was Rootie's style.

If you wanted to be Rootie's friend, you had to run down the cliffs, too.

Rootie was smart, and you never knew what was coming next. She had about five ideas per hour.

One boiling hot Saturday in July, when kids were selling lemonade from homemade stands along the beach road, Rootie decided we should start one of our own.

"But there's a lot of competition out there," she said while we were squeezing lemons in her grandmother's kitchen. "We need an angle."

By the time we had set up our stand on the road, Rootie had it all figured out.

When fat people on mopeds came along, Rootie would yell, "Get your ice cold, refreshing fruit beverage!" They'd usually hit the brakes.

To tired-looking people on bikes, she shouted, "High-energy citrus drink—better than Gatorade!"

And when sweaty joggers and grim-looking health freaks came running by, Rootie called out, "Get your pure all-natural vitamin C—help prevent scurvy!" They practically *all* stopped.

"What's scurvy?" I whispered to Rootie when the first runner was drinking his lemonade.

"It's a disease sailors got in the old days when they went for years without any vitamin C," Rootie said.

By the end of the day, we'd cleared thirty-four bucks.

Score!

Sometimes we hung out at Mrs. Bowditch's house. It was a cool place with pictures of birds on the walls. The floors tilted this way and that way, and in every room you could hear the ocean. The furniture was old—most of it was missing something, like an arm on a wooden chair, or a knob on a drawer, or a leg of a sofa (it was held up by a pile of books)—and the place smelled of dust and mold and the ocean. Everything was damp. The windows were made of little glass panes, and the curtains were brown. The pillows were brown, too. So were the rugs. Sometimes you could see a little red or blue, but I guess they had all faded. Some of the chairs were woven wicker. You had to be careful with them. The seats were mostly broken, and Mrs. Bowditch would just put a pillow over the hole. If you sat down, you could have a problem.

The walls and the ceilings were whitewashed and flaking. There were photographs hanging all crooked on the walls, and they were faded, too. I liked the ones of Mrs. Bowditch standing by one of her planes, single-engine planes with propellers twice as tall as she was. Mrs. Bowditch wore boots and riding pants and leather jackets. The coolest parts were her leather helmets and the big goggles that hung around her neck. In every picture, she was grinning. Maybe she was saying, "If you think you could fly around the world solo, why don't you try it?"

Some other pictures showed her in nightclubs with different men. Some might have been movie stars. Sometimes you could see a little ashtray on the table. Stork Club, it said.

I asked Rootie, "Where are her husbands?"

"She threw them out," said Rootie. "With the trash."

Rootie and her grandmother were a lot alike.

Rootie and I built a tree house in my backyard. That's where we hid when Looney Tunes came. I had missed going to the boat, and that was the day, of course, that Looney Tunes came. After he shot my father, he came thundering out of the house and searched the woods until he found the tree house where Rootie and I were hiding. He climbed the stick steps, and his hand came up over the platform, then his horrible face—and then the step broke, and Looney Tunes fell backward, out into the sky. We heard a crack, and when we peeked over the edge of the platform, Looney Tunes was spread out on a rock, dead.

After that, the running with my father was all over. The U.S. marshals took him away and put him in the witness protection program. I had no idea where he went. He just disappeared.

Mrs. Bowditch said I could stay with her and Rootie in New York. So, in early September, we moved there.

Mrs. Bowditch had a whole house of her own on East

64th Street. You couldn't get much fancier than that. Your own house. In that neighborhood maids walked the dogs around and doormen in uniform ran out to open the doors of taxis.

Rootie showed me around the house.

You had to push a bunch of buttons at the front door to get in. If you didn't do it just right, the security alarm would go off—silently. Then the security men would come tearing down the street in their cars. You'd better have a good reason to be standing there pushing buttons.

Downstairs was a kitchen, and a dining room that looked out on a garden with a high wall around it. A staircase curved around up to a living room, which was really big. Piano, fireplace, flowers, paintings on the walls, big fat sofas—it was a ball-buster of a living room.

There was a nice picture of the ocean over the fireplace. Green waves. It looked like Cutlass Island.

"That's a Homer," said Rootie.

"Homer who?" I said.

"Winslow Homer," she said. "Great American painter. Seascapes mostly."

I looked out the big windows at the end of the room. They looked over the garden. There were other houses all around, and they each had a garden.

"This is a fancy place," I said to Rootie. "How come Mrs. Bowditch's house on Cutlass Island is so old and falling apart?"

"That's the way she likes it," said Rootie. "So do I. Don't you?"

"Yeah," I said. "I do."

On the same floor was a library with books up to the ceiling and some portraits. One was a little girl in a white dress with blue ribbons.

"Who's that?" I said.

"Grandma," she said. "Isn't it cool?"

It was hard to see the little girl growing up to fly bombers across the ocean in the war.

On the third floor were the bedrooms and bathrooms. Rootie and her grandmother each had a room. Then, on the fourth floor, up a narrow staircase, was a small room and a bathroom. That was where I was going to live.

I liked it. It had a skylight overhead. You couldn't see through it, just yellow light. An iron ladder went up to a trapdoor in the roof.

"Can I go up there?" I said.

"If you don't tell anybody," said Rootie, "and if nobody sees you. I go up there a lot. I figured out how to fix the alarm so it never goes off."

I couldn't wait to try that trapdoor.

I thought Rootie and I were going to have a really great time in New York. I thought it would be like a giant Cutlass Island with a whole bunch of places to explore together. Except it would be sort of reversed—this time, I would be the one who knew a lot of stuff.

Rootie didn't know squat about New York. I asked her a few questions, and I found out some amazing things. She had never been to the Bronx (except to the Bronx Zoo). She had never been to Queens (except to catch a plane). She had never been to Brooklyn, period. Staten Island, period. No subway. Only buses. Lots of taxis.

I couldn't believe it. "You have never been anywhere," I said.

Rootie got pissed. "I didn't have all the advantages you had, big shot," she said. "I mean, I was never a criminal running from the law."

Well, that was the beginning of our first argument. Later on, we had bigger ones. But that was the one that started the crack in the glass.

CHAPTER 6

The Baxter School for Boys

"Tell me, young man," said Dr. Cranehill. "What are your hobbies?" His eyes squinted behind his glasses. I guess he thought we were finally on a topic I could talk about.

I couldn't think. "Sports," I said. No one could argue with sports.

"Ve-ry important," said Dr. Cranehill.

I thought I was off the hook. Wrong.

"What sports, Peter?" he said, rubbing his hands together. Dr. Cranehill was the head of the Baxter School for Boys. Mrs. Bowditch and Rootie had taken me for an interview.

"I've done a lot of running," I said.

Rootie started to cough.

"Cross-country?" said Dr. Cranehill.

"Yes, cross-country."

Rootie coughed harder.

"Wait in the hall, Rosalie," said Mrs. Bowditch.

Dr. Cranehill stood up. He was a little tub of a man. He took off his glasses, folded them up, and put them in his pocket. "Peter here seems like a promising fellow," he said. "Granted, he's a good deal behind academically, but I think he can catch up if he's willing to put his nose to the grindstone. Don't mind a little hard work, do you, Peter?"

I shook my head.

"Good fellow," he said, and whacked me on the back. "Wait outside now, so I can have a word with your grandmother."

Rootie was sitting on the stone steps of a big staircase, looking bored. A couple of boys in blue coats and neckties came by, pushing each other toward her, giggling. "Beat it, you little peckerheads," said Rootie. They ran off squealing.

"Why can't I go to your school, Rootie?" I said. "This place is a dump."

"It *is* a dump," she said. "But it's a very excellent dump for social-climbing rich people who have kids they can't get into a good private school—and would die rather than go to a public school."

"Oh," I said. "Great."

Rootie said, "You've missed a lot of school. That's not your fault, Pete."

"I don't even want to go to school," I said.

Mrs. Bowditch came out with Dr. Cranehill. "Good news, Peter," she said. "Dr. Cranehill is making a special exception for you."

"Welcome to Baxter," said Dr. Cranehill, putting out his hand.

"What do you say, Peter?" said Mrs. Bowditch.

"Thank you," I said.

So I went to Baxter School for Boys. Rootie went back to her old school—the Waverly School. Everybody in her school was really smart. Everybody in my school was a couple of beats behind the melody.

I hated the place right away. It looked like a castle. We had to wear little blue jackets with crests on the pocket.

The work was hard. In class, I could never pay attention. It drove teachers nuts.

"I'm going to explain this one more time, Peter," Mrs.

Ronson would say. "We'll go step by step. Look at me, Peter!" The other kids would start laughing.

"Yes, Mrs. Ronson."

"Don't look away. Step one—are you listening? Step one is . . ." She explained it slowly.

"Uh-huh," I'd say, every so often. "Uh-huh."

"Understand? Do you really understand?"

"Yes, I do."

"We're not going on to step two until you're positive you've got it."

"I've got it."

"He's got it," whispered the other kids, laughing. "Oh, *right.*"

"Step two," she would say.

And that was the last thing I'd hear. The teacher's voice went on and on.

Suddenly the voice stopped.

"What?" I said.

"I said, will you please explain it to the class?"

I broke into a sweat. The class started pounding their feet. I tried laughing at myself, hoping I could be part of the joke. That made it worse.

"Report for extra help after school, Peter," she would say.

During lunch, I'd walk around by myself, trying to steer clear of the kids who laughed at me. But they'd find me. They always found me.

"Hey, B.B.!" It was a skinny redheaded kid. He was standing with a bunch of other kids. "Yeah, you!"

I turned around.

"Don't you know what B.B. means?"

"He's too stupid."

"It means Bird Brain." They all hooted.

"What?" I said.

"Bird Brain!" shouted the redheaded kid.

"Tweet, tweet!" sang another kid.

My face was getting hot. I went over to the redheaded kid.

"Are you trying to mess with me?" I said quietly.

"Mess with you?" the kid said. He turned to his friends. "What an asshole!" They all hooted.

The redheaded kid turned back. He was sneering. He spit on the ground. I took a deep breath.

His eyes got wide and his mouth fell open when he saw my shoulder drop and my arm go back. He knew what was coming by then, but he didn't have a chance to get out of the way. The punch caught him square under the chin and snapped his head back. His body lifted into the air, then he fell on the pavement. *Thud.*

Everybody started yelling and running around. My fist hurt a lot, but I didn't want anybody to know.

"Anybody else?" I said.

"Geezt," said a kid. "What did you do that for? He was just kidding."

"You coulda killed him," said another.

"What a punch," said a big kid.

A teacher named Mr. Pinckney came over and grabbed me by the collar of my blue jacket. "I saw that, young man—and you've got yourself in a bunch of trouble!"

I got put on probation.

"You're hanging by a thread, young fellow," said Dr. Cranehill. "A very thin thread."

But after that nobody ever laughed at me or called me names. That's all it took: one punch.

I had to give my father credit for that. He taught me how to fight. "You don't just hit," he said. "You punch through. Boom-*boom.* Like Sugar Ray Robinson. He always got two punches for the price of one. Boom-*boom!*"

That night I waited to tell Rootie. Rootie was always on the phone with her friends, so I had to wait for a long time. At last she hung up. When I told Rootie what had happened, I thought she was going to be impressed.

I was wrong.

"That's a lousy thing to do to somebody," she said. "Why did you do that?"

"Hey," I said. "I'm not going to stand there while a bunch of punks insult me."

"Oh, macho," said Rootie. "Very macho."

"What did you want me to do? Report him to the guidance counselor?"

"What's with you, Pete—you want to get thrown out of school?" she said.

"I don't care if I do," I said. I was mad at her for not taking my side. "It's a dump."

"What'll you do then?"

"I'll go find my father, wherever he is. We did okay together."

I ran upstairs to my room. I guess thinking of my father was the last straw. I slammed the door.

CHAPTER 7

Wanted

School got worse. The work was way over my head. Every day there was a whole bunch of new stuff to learn, I didn't even try to get it. I was sure I couldn't learn. It was like a tornado of numbers and dates and facts whirling around. If a teacher asked me a question, I just broke out in a sweat.

But the other kids didn't laugh at me. Not anymore.

They didn't speak to me, either. When they saw me coming, they just drifted away. I was getting really lonely. It was worse than the old days with my father. I didn't expect anything then. But now there were kids all around all the time, having fun together. But they wouldn't even look at me. When school got out one afternoon, I decided I'd try to catch Rootie on her way home from Waverly.

Waverly was a really fancy school. Rootie's mother

and her grandmother had gone there. It was a very tough place to get into, but Rootie was a shoo-in.

It was only about six blocks to Waverly. Rootie was coming down the sidewalk with a bunch of friends. They were laughing and having a great old time. You could tell that Rootie was really popular—the boys tried to get next to her as she walked.

When Rootie saw me, she seemed a little surprised. "Hey, Pete," she said. "Where are you going?" The other kids quit horsing around. They stared at me.

I knew right away I wasn't welcome. "I'm going to Tower Records," I said. "Check it out."

Rootie introduced me to her friends. Bobby. Laura. Douglas. Sherry. Freddy. Whatever.

There was silence—just a few seconds—where Rootie would have had time to ask me to go along with them.

It didn't happen.

"See you later," I said. I hurried away down the street. Behind me, I heard them laughing and fooling around.

Then I heard Rootie call. "Hey, Pete! Wait!" I turned around. She was running toward me.

I figured she had changed her mind.

"Do me a huge favor, will you, Pete?" she said. "When

you get to Tower, could you get me a CD of the new Smashing Pumpkins? Freddy says it's slamming." She handed me a twenty. "You're a pal!"

She ran back to her friends.

Pals?

I was so mad I didn't know what to do. I kicked a garbage can. It wrecked my toe. Yow.

I limped around all afternoon, zigzagging from one street to another. I went to the park, and it was full of people playing football, flying kites, guys and their girlfriends walking together, dogs running around barking and chasing one another. Everybody having fun together.

I got out of there as fast as I could.

Next thing I knew I was going up Central Park West, and there at 79th Street was the big old Museum of Natural History. All around it were hundreds of kids going in, coming out.

I went down the block, and there was a public school on Columbus. School was letting out and the yard was packed with children, shouting and having a great time.

I went up Columbus. When I saw the mail trucks

parked on 83rd Street, I turned and headed for the post office. It was a stupid thing to do. Not that it was really dangerous or anything; it was just sort of pathetic.

I went to the post office. There were a lot of people standing in line, holding packages and things. The line went one way, then turned back and went the other. People were grumbling, and the post office employees were snapping back at them. One old guy was ranting about how inefficient they were—he was going to write his congressman.

Nobody was paying any attention to me. I drifted over to the bulletin board, just a kid loafing in the post office. I read some of the notices—new regulations, opening and closing times on certain days, holidays, new stamps issued—and then eased over to the holder with a fat stack of WANTEDS.

I flipped the cards. The faces stared out at me. EMBEZZLEMENT, ATTEMPT TO DEFRAUD, MURDER, RAPE, ROBBERY. One face after another—angry, beaten, cocky, hopeless, some looking as if they just had no idea what was going on. And once in a while, a face that was just plain deadly evil—so terrifying I shut my eyes before turning the page.

UNLAWFUL FLIGHT TO AVOID PROSECUTION AND CONFINEMENT. GRAND LARCENY.

There it was. My father's. They had never bothered to take it down. He was a lot younger. He looked defiant. *Try and get me.* He was sharp looking, not the flabby, bitter face I knew.

They had the description wrong. His eyes weren't blue. they were green. Sometimes light, sometimes dark, but green.

That night, before dinner, I sat in the library, waiting for Rootie to get home.

"Hey, Pete!" she yelled, coming up the stairs.

I didn't answer.

"Where are you?" she called.

I let her find me in the library. I just sat there, not saying anything.

"Did you find the CD?" she asked.

I pulled her twenty out of my pocket and tossed it at her. It landed on the fancy rug.

"Tell Freddy to go get his own CDs," I said. "I'm not an errand boy."

"Oh, I see," said Rootie. "It's like that."

"It's exactly like that," I said. "Don't ask me any favors."

"Like I haven't done you any favors?" she sa
way, I thought you and I could listen to the CD together. That's why I wanted it."

"Oh, right," I said. "Don't pretend I'm your big buddy. It's not like that anymore."

"What do you mean?" said Rootie.

"You've got your friends here in the city. You go to school with them, you hang out with them, you talk to them all night on the phone. I'm not part of that."

"So?" said Rootie. "They're old friends of mine. Just because you have no friends, does that mean I can't have any?"

"I don't want any. And that includes you. Just don't pretend you're my friend."

I got up and kicked the twenty.

"Don't tell me what to do," she said. "If I want to be your friend, that's my business." She looked like she might be going to cry.

I marched out of the library.

Mrs. Bowditch was in the living room, reading. She looked up as I passed the door.

"Hello, Peter, old boy," she said. "How's everything?"

"Fine," I said, and went up the stairs.

The glass was shattering now.

CHAPTER 8

Saratoga

Before Cutlass Island, before Rootie, I guess I never had an actual friend. Now I was going to lose the one I had. My father and I had always moved too fast. A month here, a week there, sometimes just days.

If I went to school, it wasn't for long. My father had taught me to be very wary of people and to keep my distance. That didn't help in trying to make friends. After school, my father would grill me. Who had talked to me? Had they asked any questions? What did they say?

Kids figured I was a loner, and they left me alone.

Since I didn't know how to make friends, I took pride in being a tough guy who didn't need anybody. Like Clint Eastwood. A high plains drifter. Come into town with his cool hat and his poncho, squinting in the sun. Everybody backed away. They knew he was dangerous.

The joke was, nobody thought I was Clint Eastwood. Or dangerous.

They just thought I was a jerk.

I got used to being by myself all the time. I thought I was okay. Then loneliness sneaked up and hit me from behind.

I wasn't prepared. I didn't have any defense.

The truth was, I wanted to own a dog. Any kind of dog.

Everywhere we went, I looked at the dogs that people had. I'd say to myself, there, that's the kind of dog I want. A big furry dog, you can't even see its eyes. Then I'd see another kind: a lean, fast dog—you could really have fun with a dog like that.

What was amazing, the way things worked out, was I got my wish. At least for a while.

My father got work one summer a couple of years back at a place called Oklahoma. Oklahoma wasn't the state. Oklahoma was at Saratoga, New York, where there was a famous racetrack.

Maybe my father got the job because he knew gamblers

in the old days. Maybe one of them did him a favor and fixed him up with some work. I don't know. But we lived in a broken-down trailer outside of town, and every day when it was still dark we'd drive in to Oklahoma.

It was foggy in the morning. You couldn't see much. We drove very slowly with the headlights on. Maybe you could see a white fence. Big trees overhead. Then, out of the fog, just ahead of us, a guy would walk across the dirt road leading a horse—and disappear.

We'd park by a low building and get out of the car. The trees were dripping. You could smell a rich smell—maybe wet straw and horse manure. Even though you couldn't see, you could hear, and I remember the one sound I heard that first day.

Soft drumming.

Boomada-boomada-boomada-boomada-boomada.

Getting louder. Then fading away.

A galloping horse. A sound I'd only heard in cowboy movies.

Then another one.

Boomada-boomada-boomada-boomada.

Oklahoma was a huge dirt track with rows of old wooden stables all around it. I don't know why it was called Oklahoma. Maybe because it was stuck far off behind the fancy racetrack. . . . like "out West."

Oklahoma was where the horses lived during the racing season. My father's job was to muck out the stables for one of the horse owners. The guy had a bunch of horses, so there was plenty of manure and plenty to do. I helped.

You took a pitchfork and shoveled manure out of the stable—that was the main thing. You tried not to scoop up too much straw; straw was pretty expensive. Then you carried the manure away in a wheelbarrow.

After that you put down fresh straw. You carried a bucket of water and hung it on the wall. You helped wash blankets and clean the tack—the reins and all the leather. You did whatever you were told to do by the trainer and the groom.

As the fog began to drift away and the sun came in low under the trees, Oklahoma came to life.

Owners drove up in their shiny Jeeps. Trainers stood by the rail holding stopwatches and clocked the horses running on the track. Guys moved up and down the alleys between the stables, pushing the wheelbarrows piled with hay or straw. Horses stuck their heads out of the stalls and looked around. Hot-walkers cooled off the horses after they ran, leading them around and around. Jockeys talked to their horses in low voices. One of them sang to his horse in Spanish.

The jockeys were awesome. A lot of them were only as tall as me, and young, too, but they were smart and brave. They could crouch up there on a horse's shoulders, six feet above the ground, holding on with only their knees while the horse went pounding along at thirty miles an hour.

At the top of the scale, above everything and everybody else—even the owners—were the horses. They were what it was all about. They were champions descended from champions. When one of them came out from the stable with its rider, led by a groom, everybody stepped out of the way, making room for royalty. The horses—tall, gleaming, mysterious—seemed to know that.

At the other end of the scale, the bottom, were the dogs. Nobody knew who they were descended from. They were everywhere, and nobody paid them much attention. Sometimes I thought about how it was just fate that their legs were short and they hadn't turned out to be horses. The dogs hung around the stables, sleeping a lot of the time. Some of them were special friends of one horse or another. People gave them a scratch behind the ear or a snack as they went by.

At the stable where my father worked, White Gate Stables, there were always six or eight dogs hanging out, usually flopped down under a big tree. They were different kinds, all mixed up.

One of them was a yellow Labrador, with maybe a little German shepherd mixed in. She was called Biscuit. First I thought she was named that because of her color. Like a cookie. Wrong. She was a slow-moving, tubby dog who seemed to be pushed along by the breeze of her tail wagging. Her fur always had a lot of straw on it. She was named after Sea Biscuit—one of the fastest horses ever. It was a joke. Biscuit was a drifter—I never saw her run—she just drifted, one place to another, wagging her tail. The first time I saw her she was asleep against the big tree, and one of her ears was resting against the trunk, pointing upward.

That day, when she woke up, she came over to me, and it was like she said, you're new here? She had soft brown eyes. She looked me over. I gave her my hand. She nuzzled it. You're okay, she seemed to say. Then she ambled away and went to sleep under the tree again.

In the early afternoon, the races began over at the

racetrack. You could hear the horn doing the *ta-ta-ta-ta-ta* and waves of cheering from the crowd. But by then it was quiet at Oklahoma, and I could take Biscuit for a walk.

We walked around, looking at everything, going no place special. Biscuit just liked to sniff things. It was a sleepy time at Oklahoma. A lot of the people had been up since long before dawn, so they were dozing off while they had the chance. At one barn, a guy had leaned his chair back against the wall, tilted his hat down over his face, put his feet on an upside-down bucket, and was sleeping in the sun, his mouth hanging open. Most people went into the shade. Some guys were playing cards inside one of the stables. You'd see people's feet sticking out of cars that had the door left open for air. Others were sacked out in the horse vans.

Sometimes, after we'd walked a long way, I'd sit down against some good, big tree. Biscuit would lie down next to me, leaning against me. That's what she liked to do—be right next to me. Sometimes she'd even lie across my feet.

Then I'd listen to the crowd at the racetrack far away, and maybe I'd watch the leaves shifting around overhead, and I'd feel Biscuit against my leg, breathing, and I'd rest my hand on her warm fur. Before I knew it, I'd be asleep, too.

That was the most peaceful time of my whole life.

During the next week, I picked up some money by helping muck out at one of the other stables. When I made enough, I got a ride to town, and I went to the pet store.

What I did was buy a collar for Biscuit. She was like the other dogs—no collar. They had a bunch of different colors in the store, and I spent a long time trying to figure out what would look good.

Red was out.

Blue was nice.

Green was okay.

Brown. Maybe.

I couldn't decide.

I'd pick one up and imagine it was against Biscuit's yellow coat. Then I'd put it back and try another color. The woman who ran the store was beginning to stare at me.

I started to get in a sweat.

Hey, Pete, I said to myself. Chill. It's only a collar for a dog.

I guess the truth was, I had never bought anything for anybody before in my life.

Green.

I bought a green collar.

That afternoon, I slipped the collar over Biscuit's head, and it settled on her neck just like it had always been there. She gave a little shake, that's all. I knew she liked it. I think she was proud.

Green was the right color. Definitely.

Now Biscuit walked around the stables looking special. You could say she was the queen of Oklahoma. Oklahoma dogs, anyway.

Two days later, a steamy afternoon, I was sitting under a tree with Biscuit curled up next to me when my father came running down the alley between two stables. His shirt was soaked, and he had a wild look.

"Come on," he said, "we're going."

I stood up.

"Come *on*," he said.

I looked down at Biscuit.

"No dog," he said.

"I want to take her," I said.

"No goddamned dog," he said. "Don't you understand English?"

Biscuit was looking up at me.

"Stay here," I said.

I reached down and patted her on the head. "Goodbye, Biscuit," I said. Then I could hardly see her because tears were in my eyes, and then I was running after my father, through the stables toward our car, and the last I saw of Oklahoma was a blur as my father started the car and we skidded onto the road and out the white fence.

CHAPTER 9

Mooshy

Moosh Marshman was the kid who tipped me off about Mr. Pinckney.

Moosh was an okay guy. He was sixteen, and making his second try at ninth grade. He wasn't dumb. He just wouldn't work. "I have one of the worst cases of attention deficit disorder in the world," he said proudly.

The real reason he didn't get kicked out was his family had given a pile of money to the school, and as long as Moosh was still a student there was always the chance they'd give another hunk.

"I've got Dr. Cranehill by the short ones," he told me.

Moosh's real name was Everett, but he was called Moosh, Mooshy, Moosh Man, Moosher, or the Mushroom. He was short and fat, and his head was like a small white potato.

Moosh wore granny glasses, and his hair parted just enough to let his nose get some air. Then the hair went down to his waist. Instead of the regulation school jacket, he wore a ratty wool baja with a hood. Between his dirty T-shirt and the top of his jeans there was a naked potbelly with a belly button staring at you, kind of winking like a broken headlight. His jeans bagged down and ended under his sandals.

Moosh had a squeaky voice. He made me laugh a lot. He had a driver's license—nobody could figure out how he got it—and he liked to cruise down by the school in his family's old Lincoln, scrunched down, honking the horn. You'd be in class, and you'd hear all this honking, and you'd look out the window and there would be this old Lincoln going by—*honk, honk, honk*—without a driver.

One afternoon he invited me to his apartment to listen to some CDs.

Moosh's apartment was weird. It was huge—enormous rooms, high ceilings, long halls, a kitchen as big as a restaurant. There was practically no furniture. The kitchen sinks were full of dirty dishes, and a couple of cats were creeping around. The smell wasn't too great.

On the wall was a small black box. "See that?" said Mooshy. "Keep looking at it." He ran off. I waited.

A bell rang, and a white card dropped into sight on the box: LIVING ROOM. Then the bell rang again. LIBRARY, said the next card. Mooshy went through the rooms, ringing bells, as I watched the white cards drop.

"Want to try it?" said Mooshy, when he came back, panting.

"Sure," I said.

He took me to the dining room. "See that lump in the middle of the rug? Go step on it."

I stepped on the lump. A bell rang in the kitchen.

I went back and there was a new card: DINING ROOM.

"What are all the bells for?" I said.

"Maids and butlers," said Mooshy. "A long time ago."

"How come you don't have any furniture?" I said.

"My sister's boyfriend, Momo, has a cocaine habit," said Moosh. "First he sold the TVs, then the silver, then the paintings, and now he's down to the furniture."

"Does he live here?"

"Sometimes," said Moosh. "Right now I think he's in Aspen. I guess he sold a chair or something."

"Where's your sister?" I said.

"What is this—*60 Minutes?*" said Moosh.

"Sorry," I said. I never saw Moosh get annoyed before.

"She's in rehab," said Moosh. "And my parents practically never come here. If they stayed too long, they'd have to pay taxes. They live in Monaco and travel around. Anything else you want to know?" His face was red, and he was sort of puffing.

"No," I said.

He didn't say anything for a while. Then he said quietly, "My brother Johnny went out the window in that bedroom down the hall." He pointed. "The door's locked. Nobody goes in there. Ever."

"I'm sorry," I said. "Why did it happen?"

"LSD, man," he said.

He walked down to his room. "You want to hear some music?" he called.

Moosh's room was a mess. Grungy old futon, a landslide of CDs, open pizza box with a couple of pale, withered slices. There was no place to sit. Moosh kicked away some dirty towels and socks, like a man going through deep snow. "Have a seat," he said.

We listened to some old CDs. The best one was Michelle Shocked singing about learning how to drive a car on back roads in East Texas.

I loved that song. It wasn't like any other song. I wondered how a person could write a song as good as that. I got Moosh to play it over a couple of times.

Later on, when we'd heard enough music, I got ready to shove off.

"I meant to tell you something," said Moosh.

"What?" I said.

"You know that guy Mr. Pinckney?"

"The English teacher?"

"Yeah," said Moosh. "With the Southern accent?"

"What about him?" I said.

"He's been telling kids in school that your father is Mafia." Moosh shrugged. "That's what he's saying."

"You sure?" I said.

"I heard him. After class. He was kind of whispering to a bunch of kids. I guess the whole school knows now."

"Knows?" I said. "Knows? Just because a little bastard said so. Is that *knows?*"

"Hey," said Moosh. "I didn't say *I* believed him."

Now I could see why the kids were staying away from me. It wasn't just that I had decked a kid. It was because I was a Crime Family—like I had a disease.

How did Pinckney hear about it, anyway? It had to be Dr. Cranehill, that creep. Mrs. Bowditch probably had to tell him something about my family to get me into the school. She must have trusted him. And he must have promised he would never say a word.

I wondered how long Cranehill had managed to keep his trap shut before he started spilling his guts to Pinckney. And how long before Pinckney whispered it to the kids.

I was mad.

"Hey, Pete," said Moosh. "Don't get all worked up. It's no big deal."

"It is to me," I said. "It's nobody's business."

"They probably talk about my family all the time," said Moosh. "Get used to it."

"I don't have to get used to it," I said. "I'm going to fix that bastard."

"*Omerta,*" said Moosh. "Revenge!"

"What are you talking about?" I said.

"You know," said Moosh. "The *Godfather* movies.

They put the horse head in the guy's bed? It was Mafia revenge."

"You want a punch in the nose?" I said. "Don't talk about my family."

"I told you about *my* family," said Moosh. "What's the matter with you? You sure have a temper."

I tried to slow down. I walked around a little. When I felt better, I said to Moosh, "I'm sorry, Moosh. I didn't mean what I said. I wouldn't hit you. You're my only friend in school."

"That's okay," said Moosh.

"I'll tell you where my father is. He's in the witness protection program," I said. "I don't know where. They put him someplace, but it's secret. I don't know what he did wrong, but a guy came to kill him a few months ago. Before that, we were always moving, hiding, on the run. That's it. That's all I know."

"So you can't ever see him or talk to him or anything?" said Moosh.

"No," I said.

"You know what I think you should do about this whole school thing?" said Moosh.

"What?" I said.

"Nothing," he said. "Absolutely nothing."

"Yeah?" I said.

"It will get better," said Moosh. "Just let it go by. That's the best thing to do."

I headed home to Mrs. Bowditch's house. On the way, I thought about Mooshy's advice.

It was good advice, I decided.

I just wish I'd taken it.

C H A P T E R 10

Big Mac and Little Hot Dog

I got kicked out of the Baxter School for Boys at noon the next day.

I missed lunch, too.

You had a choice of meat loaf or macaroni and cheese. I know because I was reading the bulletin board when Mr. Pinckney came down the hall with his little bunch of groupies. They liked to hang out with him and talk about the things they had learned in class and compete to show how clever they were. Then Mr. Pinckney would make some remark, and they would all nod—yes, yes, yes, very true. It was gross.

"*Excuse* me," Mr. Pinckney said to me. "I'd like to get by?" He said "by" like "ba." Kids were coming from the other direction. I guess I *was* blocking traffic. But I wanted to see what was for dessert.

"If you don't mind," said Mr. Pinckney.

Lemon Jell-O.

"I mind," I said. "I'm reading the menu."

I wasn't planning to say that, but that's what I said.

"I didn't know he could read," said one of the kids. They all snickered.

"Want some help?" said another. They laughed again.

Mr. Pinckney grabbed my arm. "Move," he said in a loud voice. "Right now."

"You want me to move?" I said. "Look—I'm moving!"

I yanked his briefcase out of his hand and threw it as hard as I could down the hall. It sailed end over end, spilling papers all the way. It looked like a blizzard.

I walked straight out the door of the Baxter School and down the steps. The sun was shining. There was a little breeze. I was free.

I didn't feel like going back to Mrs. Bowditch's house to face the music, so I walked down to the movies on Second Avenue. There were two theaters, side by side. I went into the first one. It was in French. I saw half. When the lights came up, I still wasn't ready to go home, so I called up Moosh. He might be home. He didn't believe it was necessary to spend the whole entire day in school. But there was no answer. I hadn't been too eager to talk to him, anyway. He had told me not to make trouble at school—and look what happened. I knew that Rootie would be really mad at me, and Mrs. Bowditch would be sore, too. That left nobody to call. So I decided to walk for a while.

I went uptown and then went over toward the river. But the river was blocked off by some big hospitals. New York Hospital and Rockefeller.

Seeing a hospital always gave me a shiver. I tried not to think about it, but I couldn't stop, and my mind started running back to the time my father drove me to the dark old hospital in the country where my mother was locked up. I was young, and scared by the hospital.

But the worst thing was seeing my mother.

She didn't know who I was. Or if she did, she didn't show it. She was the saddest person I ever saw. Her hair hung down, and she sat very still, except for her hands, which she twisted and rubbed the whole time we were there.

When we left, I kissed her on the cheek, but her cheek was cold, and she didn't notice.

I never went back. I guess she's still there. Sometimes

I wished there was a phone in her room so I could call her up when I really needed to. She might pick up the phone and hold it to her ear. She wouldn't speak, but I'd hear her breathing. I'd talk to her. I hoped she'd feel happy—even though she didn't remember who it was. I hoped she would have a feeling it was somebody, long ago, she had loved.

I'd know that I was the one.

I walked back over to Second Avenue and took the bus downtown. Then I walked toward the house on East 64th Street. School still wouldn't be out, but I figured I might as well go home and get it over with. Like going to the dentist, the sooner the better.

But then I saw something strange. I was coming to the corner of Madison Avenue when a taxi pulled up and a big hefty man in dark glasses got out. A little brown dog on a leash jumped out after him. It was Big Mac and Little Hot Dog—that's what Rootie called them. Every morning Big Mac walked Little Hot Dog up and down 64th Street, and when I came home in the afternoon they were always walking again. Then, in the evening, they took another stroll.

Rootie knew about dogs, and she said Little Hot Dog

was probably part beagle—low-slung but strong, with long floppy ears.

Big Mac was not a friendly guy. All he'd ever do was nod. If you tried to pat Little Hot Dog, Big Mac would yank on the leash and pull the dog away. When he saw me, he gave a start. I wondered why. I saw him all the time. What was different?

They hurried across the street and went down 65th Street.

Then it came to me. What was different was I came home from school early. An hour early.

Big Mac knew my routine.

I watched till he was far down the block, then I crossed the street. Bernie, the skinny old super at one of the buildings, was watering flowers by the entrance.

Bernie was a nice guy. He said hello all the time. I asked him how he was doing. We talked a little pro football. He liked the Raiders. Then I said, "Who's that big guy with the little dog who's always walking along the street?"

"I don't know him," said Bernie.

"Does he live on the street?"

"No," said Bernie. "Probably in the neighborhood."

"Are you sure?" I said.

"What is this—an interrogation?" said Bernie. "I been here sixteen years. I know who lives here."

"I know you do," I said. "That's why I asked you."

"Is there a problem?" said Bernie.

"No," I said. "He just seemed strange."

"Forget it," said Bernie. "In this city, strange is no big deal."

I said good-bye and went home.

In the foyer, as Rootie called it, I waited.

Why would Big Mac walk his dog up and down our street if he didn't even live here? Why would he do it exactly when we went to school and exactly when we came home, and again when we might be going out at night?

Just then I looked out through the heavy glass of the front door. Little Hot Dog was trotting by. At the end of his leash was Big Mac. As he passed the house he turned his head slowly and looked in. I pushed against the wall. He saw me anyway, and he gave a weird smile—a creepy smile that had nothing to do with being friendly. He wasn't smiling at *me*.

Then he was gone, and I was shivering. The answer to all the questions was obvious.

Me.

CHAPTER 11

Mrs. Bowditch's Beechcraft

"So you've blotted your copybook, eh, Peter?" said Mrs. Bowditch. "I must confess I never thought you'd take to the Baxter School for Boys. Nevertheless . . ." Her voice trailed off.

"What does that mean—'blot your copybook'?" I said.

"It's from the days when students had a book in which they wrote their lessons, using a pen—the sort of pen you dip into your inkwell. It gave little boys an opportunity to make a dreadful mess. Then they would be scolded for blotting their copybook."

"Oh," I said.

"You might remember," she said, "that losing your temper—lovely as it feels—only hurts the one who does it. Is that too trite?"

I shook my head. I didn't know what trite was, but if Mrs. Bowditch said it, it was probably right.

"You and I are quite similar," she said. "Impatient and reckless, and we react much too fast to what we perceive as a slight or an injustice."

I shook my head again, though I didn't know what "slight" meant.

"I once knocked out a man in Alaska," she said. "He's probably long gone by now, and if he isn't, I'm sure he never gives a thought to the strange young woman who came down from the sky and knocked him out fifty years ago." She took a sip of sherry. "But I think of him every so often, and I feel badly."

I waited for her to go on, but she was off in Alaska, I guess. Finally I said, "Where did it happen?"

"Oh," she said. "Anchorage, I believe. It was in the late thirties, and I had a lovely red Staggerwing Beechcraft—a biplane with the lower wing slightly ahead of the upper wing. It had a 250-horsepower engine—very powerful. On takeoff you couldn't see over the engine, so you just crossed your fingers and gunned it. I adored that plane."

She sipped some sherry.

"I can't remember what time of year it was exactly, but it was bitterly cold. I had no reason to be flying in Alaska, except that my father told me not to do it. The oil in the plane's engine got thicker and thicker. I had to land and try to warm it up. I came down in this field. Nobody was around. I went into the woods and gathered some wood and made a fire. I poured the oil—which was like molasses by now—into a tin can and heated it. When it got thin, I poured it back into the engine."

"What about the guy you hit?" I said.

"It was a redneck who came along driving a jalopy. He watched me work for a while. When I finished, he invited me to climb in and get warm in his pickup. I knew it was a very poor idea, but I thought I might stay just long enough to defrost my fingers."

The phone rang. Mrs. Bowditch picked it up. "Hello?" Then she said, "Oh, hello, sweetie. Where are you? . . . Oh, sure. But do be home by nine if you can. Bye, Rootie, dear." She hung up. "That was Rootie. She's going to the movies with Freddy." I gritted my teeth.

"We'll tell Rootie about your scholastic difficulties tomorrow," she said. She got a little more sherry.

"Where were we?" said Mrs. Bowditch.

"The jalopy and the redneck?"

"Right-o," she said. "I got into the jalopy. It smelled as if every lumberjack in Alaska had stored his dirty socks in there. He asked me what a girl was doing, flying all alone in Alaska. We talked. Then he offered me a place to stay. His place. I decided it was time to get out of the jalopy. That's when he lunged at me. I grabbed my big pocket knife that was in my flying coat. I held it in the palm of my glove, and gave the fellow a splendid whack across the side of his head. That seemed to do it. When I got out of the jalopy, he was sleeping like a child. I started the Beechcraft and took off. I remember snow was beginning to fall."

"How come you're sorry you did that?" I asked. "It was his fault."

She finished off her sherry. "The poor man must have come to, splitting headache, wondering what in the world had happened—and the only clue the sound of an airplane fading away into the snowy sky. I think it's rather sad." She glanced at the clock on the mantel. "Whoops—time for the news." She headed for the library. "I'm going out to dinner after the news, Pete, so we'll have a good chat about schools first thing tomorrow.

In the meantime, don't fret. Never did anyone a bit of good."

I went down to the kitchen and made myself a sandwich. The kitchen was right up against the street. But it had bars across the windows and shades pulled down. Big Mac could be standing on the sidewalk five yards away, and you wouldn't know it. You'd be totally safe. At least for now.

I ate the sandwich, and then I went up to my room. My books from school were lying around. They were from a part of my life that was over. I used to be scared of them. Now, as I flipped through them, they seemed harmless. Parts were even interesting.

I read for a while, and I guess I fell asleep, because when I opened my eyes it was dark, except for the dull yellow windows in the tall buildings downtown. I climbed up the metal ladder and unlatched the heavy trapdoor. I climbed out on the roof.

The sky was a pink color, churning, but you could see a couple of stars in places. Standing on the roof made you feel like you were an orchestra conductor, leading the whole city.

I sat down and leaned against the chimney. It was

made of bricks, and there were places where little bubbles of tar stuck between the cracks. You could break off a piece and play with it.

I thought about Cutlass Island.

At night, Rootie and I would stand on the beach with the warm waves coming in and flowing around our feet, and the sky would be dark blue-black, splattered with stars. Rootie and I would watch as the beam from the lighthouse down at the point swung past us, reaching out across the water, then pulling back and disappearing. We could almost feel the light moving behind us on the other side of the island, and then there it was—coming around again.

I wished I was back on Cutlass Island, with Rootie, standing on the beach.

Just then, the trapdoor screeched open. "Pete," said Rootie. "We just got a call from the marshals. I'm really sorry, Pete—"

I shouted, "What happened? Tell me!"

Rootie was crying. "He was shot to death," she said. "Somewhere in Missouri."

PART II

NEW YORK

CHAPTER 12

The Sweep

After we got back from the Ozarks, I switched over to a public school.

I liked it a lot better than Baxter. It was no uptight, white-bread school. You didn't get any of that who-was-your-grandfather crap you got at Baxter. They took you as is.

The neighborhood was different—you had to be careful. A kid was stabbed on the way to school one morning. I didn't see it happen, but I did see the cops and the ambulances with their flashing lights, and a crowd of people. The medics were rolling somebody in a stretcher into an ambulance. Everybody had a different story—some said it was two older guys attacking two school kids. Others said it was one kid. Either way it was horrible.

The police had strung a red ribbon across the sidewalk

to mark the crime scene. Usually it would be one of those yellow tapes that says POLICE LINE DO NOT CROSS. But for some reason this was a red ribbon, like around a present. You couldn't go through. A bunch of people were standing up against it. I thought maybe they were looking at a body or something. I pushed through far enough to take a look. There was no body, and no bloodstains, either. Not that I saw. It was just a stretch of empty sidewalk, but in the middle was one yellow baseball cap.

I shivered when I saw that cap. There was nothing special about it, but I couldn't help thinking that half an hour ago it had been sitting on some kid's head—just as regular and ordinary as his backpack or his homework or his sneakers. All part of a plain old day, getting up and going to school.

And then a knife went into him, and now maybe he was dead.

It could happen to any kid.

I wondered if anybody was going to come and get that kid's yellow hat.

The school was huge and jammed with kids. I got to know some of them pretty fast. They were okay. The noise in the school was tremendous, bouncing off the high ceilings and echoing down the halls. Every classroom was packed, and some kids sat at desks out in the hall. Maybe they had done something wrong, but probably it was just overcrowding. The biggest noise was on the stairs—they were metal, and kids came crashing down them, yelling to one another.

I liked the teachers. Most of them. They were strong people, you could see that. Otherwise, they wouldn't last in that school. They had to keep order, they had to try to teach, they had to watch out for kids who couldn't keep up.

My favorite was Mr. Rivera. He was our homeroom teacher. He was a huge guy with at least three chins—but he wasn't tall. He was squat, and his arms were like hams. You wouldn't think he could move fast, but anybody who tested him found out different. He sometimes looked like he was half asleep, but his arm would lash out and grab a kid's shirt in a split second. Then Mr. Rivera would lift the kid between his thumb and two fingers, like he was selecting a chocolate out of a box of candy. He'd hold the kid in the air for a while, kind of studying him as if the kid was some weird creature he'd just pulled out of the water. Mr. Rivera didn't say anything, he just looked. Of course, the other kids were laughing the whole time. By the time Mr. Rivera put the kid down on his feet again, the kid would think twice about making trouble in that class.

Mr. Rivera would answer any questions you had. He was patient, and he took time with you. But mainly he never made you feel stupid.

When school got out, I'd see Mr. Rivera standing on the sidewalk, smoking a cigarette. Kids would pour out the doors and flow around him, like he was a big boulder in a river.

When the kids were mostly gone, he'd step on his cigarette and kind of waddle away. He went toward the subway. I don't know if he had a family. Maybe not.

Maybe school was his life. Maybe he was the boulder in the river.

One afternoon I was walking home from school when a car pulled up across the street from me. It was a red Geo Prizm.

"Hey, Pete!" a man called.

I kept going. I didn't know who it was. Pretended I didn't hear him.

"Hey, Pete!" he yelled again. "Slow down. It's okay."

I stopped and turned.

The guy was waving a badge at me. "U.S. marshal," he said. "Witness protection." He smiled. "It's okay," he said.

He stopped the car, double-parked, and jumped out. He was a tall, loose-jointed kind of guy, maybe like a basketball player.

He came over and stuck out his hand. "I'm Jack Farrell," he said. "Special agent. Hope I didn't give you a scare." He grinned, kind of an off-center grin.

"What do you want?" I wasn't too crazy about seeing witness-protection guys.

"I'm sorry about your dad," he said. "Everybody in the department is upset about that."

I didn't say anything.

"My assignment is to do a follow-up on families of the deceased," he said. "Check in, see how they're doing. . . . How's your new school working out?"

"Fine," I said.

"Is there anything we can do for you?" he said.

"No," I said. "I got to get home." I started walking.

Farrell caught up with me. "Listen," he said. "I realize this business has been upsetting."

"Then just leave me alone, all right?" I said. I walked faster.

"Can't do that, Pete," he said. "Fact is, we've been hearing things."

"What does that mean?" I said.

"Could you possibly stand still for a minute so I could talk to you?" he said. He grinned.

I stopped.

"We hear guys are still looking for that money your father took." I didn't say anything. "That's why they've been keeping an eye on you," he said.

"What?" I said. "Who's keeping an eye on me? Who are you talking about?"

"You haven't noticed anybody? Nothing out of the ordinary?"

"No," I said.

I thought of Big Mac and Little Hot Dog. But should I tell him? What if Farrell was a phony? I didn't know what to do.

"Maybe there's one thing," I said.

"What's that?" he said.

"I'll call you at your office," I said.

"Do that," he said. He pulled a card out of his wallet.

I looked at it. There was a Justice Department seal in gold. John G. Farrell, it said. United States Marshal. Department of Justice. Then the phone number and his extension. "Don't waste any time, Pete," he said. "Call me as soon as you can."

"Maybe I will," I said.

"I mean it," he said. Then he went back to his car, got in, and drove away.

That afternoon I called Mooshy and told him what had happened. "I don't know what to do," I said.

"You don't trust him?"

"I don't trust anybody," I said. "He seemed like a pretty nice guy, though."

"Do you think he's a mob guy?"

"Could be," I said. "How can I tell?"

"Run a test on him, Pete," said Mooshy.

"Like what?"

"First you call him at the Justice Department. Does he answer the phone? Do they know who he is?"

"Okay," I said. "What if he's there?"

"Tell him about Big Mac and Little Hot Dog," said Mooshy. "See if he comes up with anything. That'll be the test."

I did exactly what Mooshy said. I ran the test.

I took his card and called the Justice Department, and they gave me the same extension that was on his card.

"Farrell," he said.

"This is Pete," I said.

"My man!" he said. "Glad you called."

I told him about Big Mac and Little Hot Dog.

"Thanks for calling, Pete," he said. "I'll run a check on the guy. Maybe we'll talk to him. I'll give you a call in a couple of hours."

That was that.

Rootie came home around six. "Any calls?" she said.

"No," I said. "But I'm expecting one."

"Ohhhh," she said. "Want me to stay off the phone?"

"If you can," I said.

"Funny," she said. "And I thought it was my phone."

I could tell Rootie had that look in her eye. A fight was coming. Another lousy fight with Rootie.

We'd had a lot of them since we moved to New York.

Rootie was glaring at me.

"It's an important call," I said.

"Oh, is *Mooshy* calling?"

"No," I said. "But what's wrong with Mooshy? Is he not allowed to call?"

"Nothing," she said. "Just he's a total loser, and he talks forever, and I can't call my friends."

"You mean like your boyfriend Freddy? And all those other wimpo dickheads *you* run around with?"

Rootie screamed at me. "I wish you didn't live here!"

"Me, too!" I yelled.

"Why don't you get out?" Rootie shouted. "Find your own place!"

"I can't wait!" I said. "I'm gone! Hear me? I'm gone!"

And that's when the phone rang.

I grabbed it. "Hello?"

"Pete? Jack Farrell. Witness protection."

"Hi."

"How are you doing?"

"Okay," I said.

"We checked out the big guy and the little dog. He's clean. No record. Lives over by York Avenue. I stopped by and talked to him myself. Turns out he's harmless. A little weird. He walks the dog on that street because that's where he and his late wife lived twenty years ago. They had a puppy, and they used to walk it together. You know, sentimental nostalgia."

"Oh," I said. "Well, thanks for checking."

"I'm not quite finished, Pete. I'd like to sweep the

house where you're staying. Make sure there's no surveillance. If that's okay with the family."

"You think you'd find something?" I said.

"Don't know," he said, "but I'd feel more comfortable if I was sure you weren't bugged."

"I guess nobody would mind," I said.

"It's for your own good, Pete," he said. "Clear it with Mrs. Bowditch and the girl. If I don't hear from you, I'll come around about four-thirty tomorrow."

Mrs. Bowditch wasn't too crazy about having some stranger poking around her house. When Jack Farrell showed up the next afternoon, she was pretty cold and asked him a lot of questions, such as what was his opinion of "that monster" J. Edgar Hoover, the old F.B.I. boss.

I guess his answers were okay because Mrs. Bowditch offered him some tea and lemon cookies. He said no, thanks, and stood up to begin his search.

"Could you come down and turn off the burglar alarm?" he said.

"I'll do it," said Rootie.

"When I get outside, lock the door," said Farrell.

A minute later, Rootie ran back up. "He's out on the sidewalk," she said. "He'll never get back in."

"I bet he does," I said.

"He seems awfully clever," said Mrs. Bowditch.

We heard the front door slam, then steps on the stairs. Jack Farrell came in and sat down.

"Piece of cake," he said.

"How did you do it?" I said.

He took something that looked like an electric toothbrush out of his pocket. "This is called a rattler," he said. "It's an electric lock pick. It jiggles the pins, then the core gets turned—maybe ten, fifteen seconds—your lock is open."

He put it back in his pocket. "Incidentally, Pete, thanks for expressing confidence in me when I was out on the street." He grinned. "I appreciate that you bet on me."

"How did you know that?" said Rootie.

"Easy," he said. "I left my pen when I went downstairs." He picked up a fountain pen from the table next to his chair and waved it. "Of course, it's not really a pen. It's an FM wireless microphone. Runs on a couple of penlight batteries. But you guessed that, right?"

"It never crossed my mind," said Mrs. Bowditch.

He put the pen in his coat.

"The easiest thing in the world is a phone tap," he

said. "It can be done down-line—outside the house—in the telephone company junction box on the corner, or in your basement in ten minutes, or by slipping a carbon mike in one of your phone receivers."

"How would they get in?"

"If a guy was wearing a uniform and driving a telephone company truck, and told you there was a problem with your line. . . ."

"Well, in that case . . ." Mrs. Bowditch said.

"If you let somebody deliver a package, or come in to clean a rug or to pick up some dry cleaning—all he needs is a few seconds to drop a remote control transmitter, and pow, you're on the air." He looked around. "If this was an apartment, you could be bugged from the apartment next door. They could use a spike—a nail with a mike in it—and drive it partway into the wall. It would pick up everything you said or did. But since this is a private house, they couldn't do that. So what *could* they do?"

He scratched his chin as if he were trying to figure it out. "You've got a power line into your house, haven't you? Of course; everybody does. It can come in handy as a cable to the outside world. A small attachment to a wall plug, nobody notices it behind the sofa or under your bed, and right away the world is listening." He paused. "So where can you get privacy when you want to talk? How about out on the street? Wrong. A good shotgun mike will pick you up loud and clear from a hundred yards away." He grinned.

"Can you discover if we're being bugged?" I said.

"Absolutely," said Farrell. "For example, there's a scanner that will block out radio and TV, and just search for other sounds. It's all pretty expensive—microwave detectors, ultrasonic generators—but if it's an inside line tap you can probably locate it with a cheap ohmmeter, which measures the change in resistance on the line."

"Speaking for myself," said Mrs. Bowditch, "you're getting a bit ahead of me."

"Sorry, Mrs. Bowditch," said Farrell. "I was going to mention the so-called burst transmitter, but I'll skip it."

"No," said Rootie. "I want to hear."

"Well," said Farrell. "This one is a transmitter that hides itself by its own tricks. It converts sound into digital form. Then the information is stored in memory chips. It's very hard to discover the transmitter because it's not continuous. Most of the time it's silent. It only surrenders the info when you want it—in a burst." He paused. "Heard enough?"

"One more," said Rootie.

Farrell laughed. "I'll skip lasers—that's a fantastic world, but very complex. My personal favorite is the visible-light transmitter. It's used at night, or near dusk."

"What does it do?" I said.

"First, it requires a break-in. Somebody has to plant a special mike in a lamp like this one." He touched the lamp on the table beside him. "The mike picks up sound, amplifies it, and converts it into electrical impulses, varying the voltage, making the bulb get a little brighter, a little darker. The variation is so slight you wouldn't notice it even if you sat right next to it."

"So the sound of your voice is changed into light?" said Rootie.

"You got it," said Farrell. "Then somebody in one of those buildings there"—he pointed across the backyard—"has a telescope trained on the lamp in your living room. It focuses on your little light bulb here, and a receiver converts the changing light from this bulb back into sound. The guy can hear exactly what you're saying as clearly as if he were sitting on that sofa."

"Neat," said Rootie.

Farrell got to his feet. "I'm going to make a sweep of the house now. Won't take long. If there's anything here, I'll find it." He smiled. "I think you'll feel a little more secure."

He was out of the room then, carrying his briefcase. We all just looked at one another.

"Remarkable," said Mrs. Bowditch at last.

In twenty minutes he was back. "All clear," he said with a big smile. He shook hands with Mrs. Bowditch and said good-night. "See you, Pete, Rootie," he said. "Let me know if anything unusual happens, will you? Anything at all?"

Mrs. Bowditch nodded. "I shall," she said.

"Take care, Pete, and stay in touch."

Then Farrell was gone.

CHAPTER 13

Letter from Missouri

That night after dinner, I was in my room packing my stuff when Rootie came to the door.

"I keep thinking about that Farrell guy," she said. "It's scary how somebody could be listening to us in this house, and we wouldn't even know it."

"It doesn't make much difference to me," I said. "I'm moving out."

"Oh, yeah?" said Rootie. "Since when?"

"Didn't you just tell me you wanted me to get out?" I said.

"I guess I did," she said. "I didn't realize how soon you'd leave."

I didn't say anything.

"Where are you going to go?" said Rootie.

"I called Mooshy. He said I could stay there for a while. He's got plenty of room."

"What's the big rush?" said Rootie.

"I don't want to be where people don't want me," I said. "I'm tired of fighting with you. It's practically like living with my father again."

"Well, I don't like it, either," said Rootie. "But you act so lousy."

"So do you," I said. "Ever since we came to the city, you don't want anything to do with me. You've got all your old friends and everything."

"Is that my fault?" said Rootie. "Or is it your fault?"

"I don't know," I said, "but you and I were special friends—out on Cutlass Island."

"We were," she said. "Definitely."

"I guess that's over," I said.

"If you say so," said Rootie.

We didn't look at each other or say anything after that. What was there to say?

When I looked up, Rootie was gone.

I felt sick. Like after a ride on a roller coaster.

I started balling up my clothes and throwing them into the suitcase. Shirt. Sweater. Sneakers. Pants—

Something crinkled in my hand. Something in the back pocket of my old jeans.

Maybe it was money.

I reached in and pulled out a letter.

It was the letter from my father.

It must have been there ever since Mr. Creech had handed it to me that day in the Ozarks.

I didn't want to read it then, and I didn't want to read it now.

Especially now, after what had just happened with Rootie.

The envelope was all crumpled. There was no name on it. Just a plain envelope, stained and dirty.

Mooshy once told me you could read a letter without opening it. He said you spray the envelope with a can of Freon. The envelope turns transparent for a little while, and you can read the letter right through it. When the Freon dries, the envelope turns back into an ordinary envelope again. Nobody knows you read the letter.

I didn't have any can of Freon. Otherwise that's what I would have done. Just read part of the damn letter through the envelope, then thrown the whole thing away.

Why couldn't my father just leave me alone? Wasn't it bad enough when he was alive?

I ripped the envelope open. Three sheets of paper. One was a small, weird-looking drawing. My father's handwriting was kind of hard to read. I guess he never wrote much in his whole life, except maybe a few post-cards. The letter was blurred in places. He must have used a busted ballpoint.

Dear Pete—
How is that old pal of mine? They don't let me phone or write, that's why you haven't heard. But I miss you all the time, Pete.

I don't know when I will ever see you again. Who knows. If I cooperate and testify for the govt. they say I will get off with a light sentence or maybe go free. But that is down the road. I am pretty sure others will try to prevent me from testifying in the 1st place.

I am going to tell you something VERY IMPORTANT. It is SECRET. I will give it to a trusted friend in case anything happens to me. Only you can figure it out. It has a poem so you can memorize it. When you memorize the poem, BURN IT.

Then do what it says to do. Its for your own good.

I hope you are doing O.K. Pete. A lot of nights

I cant sleep because I think about you and how I was lets face it a lousy Dad. But you know that dont you better than anybody. If I could go back and change it now jesus I would. But too late now. Whats done is done. I love you, Pete. You were the one good thing in my life. Last night I was sitting on the porch late and looking at the mountains here. Then when I finally got to bed I had a dream you and I were walking together down a street on a steep hill. Maybe it was in that town up the Hudson River—remember—where we could see those big mountains on the other side, and we saw that freight train go by? Maybe 135 cars we counted. You said 140. I said 135. Anyways we were together. You and me.

In the dream, I mean. Like old days.

Your Dad.

I put the letter down on the bed.

I wished I had written him a letter just once. When I had the chance.

After a while, I picked up the poem:

The small house next to the big house
Had an orange rug on the ground.
You didn't like that kind of music
You dig Rock am I right?

It was a crappy poem, and it didn't make any sense. The drawing on the third sheet was worse.

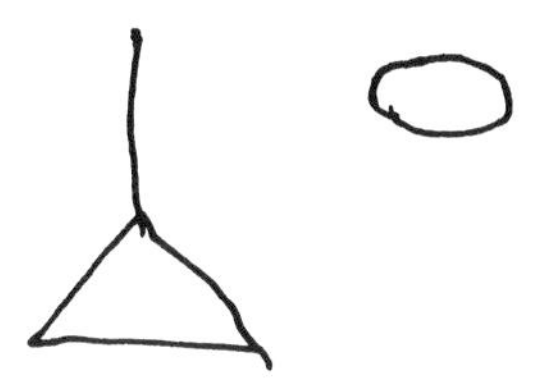

What was it, anyway? A flying saucer coming down on a tent? Was my father trying to drive me nuts?

Big house. Small house. Rug. Music. Rock.

The whole thing was such a drunk idea—write a secret code that the bad guys wouldn't be able to figure out. And just to make sure, make it so dense that your own son can't read it. Good thinking, Dad.

But I knew it was important—that much was clear. I had to figure it out somehow.

I guess I forgot that Rootie and I were in a big fight—the worst so far. I went to the top of the stairs.

"Rootie!" I yelled. "Come here! I need you!"

"It's pretty obvious that 'you dig' means just what it says," Rootie said half an hour later. "You get a shovel and you dig."

"Right," I said.

"'You didn't like that kind of music'—any idea about that?"

"I don't know," I said. "There's a lot of music I don't like."

"We'll go back to that," said Rootie. "How about 'orange rug on the ground'?"

"No idea."

" 'Big house' and 'small house' . . . Where's that?"

I shrugged. "Missouri, maybe?"

"Maybe," said Rootie. "He would have had plenty of time out there."

"Mr. Creech told me my father boasted he had buried millions of dollars someplace," I said. "Mr. Creech thought it was a joke."

"Maybe your father buried it near his cabin," said Rootie. "And whoever tore up the cabin that day was looking for it."

"But it says 'small house.' Did you see a small house out there?"

"I wasn't paying much attention."

"How can we find out?"

"Why don't we call Mr. Creech in Missouri?" said Rootie. "He'd know."

"It's pretty late—almost ten," I said. "The old guy's asleep."

"It's not that late out in Missouri; it's a different time zone," said Rootie. "Come on."

We ran downstairs to the living room.

You could hear the television going in the library. Mrs. Bowditch liked to watch a crime show on Friday nights. Mrs. Bowditch would doze off while the guns were firing and the people screaming and the cars crashing—you'd see her sleeping peacefully in her big chair, her hands folded in her lap.

Rootie called Missouri information. Rootie didn't have to write the number down. That's how she was. She just dialed it. Then she handed me the phone.

It rang three times, then a man answered. "Hello?" It was not an old man's voice.

"Hello," I said. "Is Mr. Creech there?"

"This is Mr. Creech," he said. It was like he was bracing himself for one of those phone solicitations.

"Can I help you?" he was getting ready to hang up.

"I think I've called the wrong Mr. Creech," I said. "Is there another Mr. Creech in the town—an older man, lives in a cabin?"

"Not anymore," he said.

"Did he move away?" I said.

"Who is this?" said Mr. Creech.

I told him who I was, and how Mr. Creech was a friend of my father's.

"I see," said Mr. Creech. He sounded like a banker or a businessperson.

"Do you know where I could find Mr. Creech?" I said.

"Mr. Creech died three weeks ago in an accident. His cabin burned down."

"Oh, no," I said. I could see the old guy so clearly now. "I'm sorry."

"He was my cousin. Not that we were close, really. But it's a very sad situation. Very sad."

The guy didn't sound so broken up he couldn't handle it. Old Creech was probably just an embarrassment to the other Creeches in town. I said good-bye.

I told Rootie.

"You're kidding," she said. "The poor guy. He was a nice old person."

"Yeah," I said. "I liked him a lot."

"He was a good friend to your father," she said. "His best friend."

"His only friend," I said.

"They say it was an accident?"

"Yes," I said. "Do you believe that?"

Rootie thought for a minute. "Seeing as how he drank a lot, I'd say there's a ten percent chance it was an accident."

"I'd say five," I said. "I'll bet it was murder."

"Me, too," said Rootie.

We didn't speak for a minute. Then Rootie said, "You know what, Pete?"

"What?"

"I feel like people out there are closing in on us," said Rootie quietly, as if somebody might be listening. "We don't even know who they are, but every day they're getting closer." She grabbed my arm. "Should I be getting scared?" Her fingers dug into my arm.

CHAPTER 14

Looney Tunes' Rug

Around midnight, we burned the letter and the poem and the drawing, just the way my father had told me to do, because by then Rootie and I had figured it all out.

We crumpled the papers and stuck them in the fireplace and set fire to them. We watched the flames eat them up, creeping through the paper, until there was nothing left but a small black ball of ashes and a thin trail of white smoke drifting up the chimney. I tried not to think of Creech's cabin burning.

The puzzle had gotten solved fast when Rootie said, "Let's try Cutlass Island for a while."

"Okay," I said. "'The small house next to the big house . . .'"

"That could be my grandmother's house," said Rootie. "There's a little gardening shed next to it."

"He wouldn't go digging over there," I said. "People might see him."

"So maybe it would be his own place? Where he could keep an eye on the road?"

"Sure," I said, "but where's the small house?"

"Let's look at the drawing again," she said.

We stared at the tent and the flying saucer.

"What's that pole sticking up from the tent?" said Rootie. "A flagpole?"

"Where's the flag?" I said. "Maybe it's an aerial. Maybe it's at the Coast Guard station."

"Maybe," said Rootie slowly, "it's just upside down." She turned the paper around. "What do you see now?"

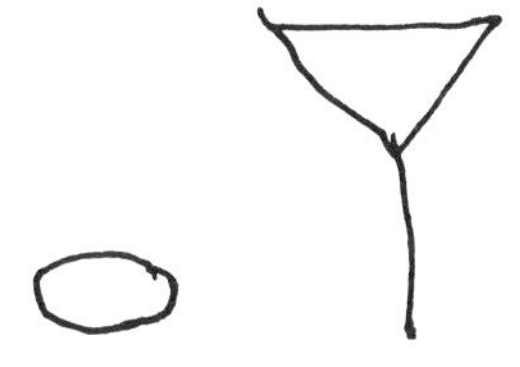

"I see a big potato next to a telephone pole," I said. "That's a big help."

"Don't be in such a hurry, Pete," said Rootie. "We're doing fine."

"Could that potato be something else?" I said. "Like a big rock?"

"The poem says, 'You dig Rock am I right?' " said Rootie. "Let's think of it as a rock for a minute—a rock where you dig."

"But where *is* the rock?" I said. "There are a thousand rocks and a thousand telephone poles on Cutlass."

"He didn't say telephone pole," said Rootie. "He said small house."

"But it looks like a telephone pole," I said.

"It also looks like one of those platforms people build so that the hawks, the ospreys, can make a nest," said Rootie. "There's a bunch of them down by the marsh."

"Platform," I said. " 'Small house.' "

"Tree house," said Rootie softly.

"Tree house," I said. "You got it."

"*Score,*" said Rootie. Then she was talking fast. "It's our tree house—the small house next to the big house. Where we hid when Looney Tunes came—"

"Yeah— Looney Tunes! 'You didn't like that kind of music. . .' "

" 'Had an orange rug on the ground'—I don't remember any rug," said Rootie. "We put a chair and a table up in the tree house. But a rug on the ground?"

"Orange rug," I said. "What's another word for rug?"

"Carpet?" said Rootie.

"What did Looney Tunes have on his head?"

"A hat?"

"No—"

"That horrible-looking hairpiece?" said Rootie.

"Some people call that a toupee," I said. "That's the polite word. But when nobody's around, people call it a rug."

"It was orange," said Rootie. "Sort of pink-orange. Really gross."

"And when Looney Tunes fell from the tree and hit his head on the rock, the rug flew off. He was bald as an egg."

"He looked better without it—even if he was dead," said Rootie.

"I remember looking at that thing—it was lying on the ground—and thinking it looked like roadkill."

"We've got it now, Pete," said Rootie. "The whole thing. We don't even have to memorize the poem."

That's when we burned the letter.

"We have to get to Cutlass now," said Rootie. "Fast. The morning boat."

I said, "Right—but how do we leave New York without anybody knowing? What about school? What about your grandmother? What about Mr. Farrell?"

"I don't know," said Rootie. "Incidentally, why didn't Farrell tell us about Creech?"

"He probably never heard of Creech," I said. "He wasn't in Missouri."

"You'd better tell him right away," said Rootie. "I'd feel safer if he knew."

"I'll call him in the morning," I said.

"Okay," said Rootie. "Now suppose we can sneak out of the city—how do we catch the ferry to Cutlass?"

"That's a problem," I said. "It's three hours away."

"We'll need to catch the early boat," said Rootie, "so we can dig up whatever it is and still catch the afternoon boat back."

"We need a car," I said.

"And a driver," said Rootie.

"Should we ask Farrell?"

"Are you kidding?" said Rootie. "If we tell him about this, the entire Justice Department will be landing on Cutlass tomorrow—probably by helicopter. They'll dig up that yard with backhoes, and we'll be completely cut out of the whole thing."

"You're right," I said. "We can tell Farrell what we found after we've found it."

"If we want to," said Rootie with a grin.

"Yeah," I said. "If." I couldn't help grinning myself.

"Should we ask Grandma to drive us?" said Rootie. "She's an old pilot. She likes adventure."

"At five in the morning?" I said. "And what do we tell her—we want to go for a picnic on Cutlass?"

"I'll leave her a note," said Rootie. "A school trip, or something."

We sat and thought for a while.

"I have a last resort," I said.

"Who?" said Rootie.

"Mooshy," I said.

"No, no, no," said Rootie. "Not a chance. No way. Never."

"He might do it," I said.

"You think I'd get in a car with that guy driving?" said Rootie. "Think again."

"He's got wheels."

"Wheels in his head," said Rootie. "And spinning."

"No," I said. "He's got a car."

"He's got some ancient junker his father threw away," said Rootie. "You told me."

"It's a Lincoln Continental," I said. "Convertible. Very cool."

"It's an antique," said Rootie. "A wreck."

"Mooshy is good at fixing things," I said.

"Mooshy can't even pull up his own pants," said Rootie.

"You don't know Mooshy," I said. "Mooshy is a good guy, and he'll drive us to the ferry."

"Do we split the treasure with him?" said Rootie. "Or just pay for the gas?"

"You know," I said, "you're sounding kind of greedy and possessive about this. It's not your treasure in the first place."

"Is it yours?" said Rootie. "I hadn't heard that. I thought it was stolen."

Rootie was right. As usual.

"I'm calling the Moosh," I said. I picked up the phone.

"Is he awake at this hour?" asked Rootie.

"Definitely," I said. "This is his best time. After Letterman, during the escort ads, and before the late late movie."

I dialed his number. After about five rings, the answering machine came on.

"Moosh residence," said Mooshy's voice.

"It's me—Pete," I said. "Are you asleep? Where are you? Hey, Moosh, do you want to give us a ride to Cutlass

Island early tomorrow morning? We have to dig up some buried treasure."

"Don't tell him that!" yelled Rootie.

"Forget that last part, Moosh—the part about the buried you-know-what," I said. "Call us back, okay? This is serious."

I slammed down the phone. "Where could he be?" I said.

Just then, I had a weird sense that something was wrong. I didn't know what. But something was wrong.

I had heard a sound.

I picked up the phone receiver again. The phone was old and black—the kind where you put your fingers in the holes and dial the number. Mrs. Bowditch was not about to get some modern pastel touch-tone phone. She liked what she was used to. She dialed with the wrong end of a pencil. That was her style.

I slammed the receiver down again the way I had done before. And there was the sound—a loose sound, sort of a rattle. I unscrewed the mouthpiece.

The bug was sitting in there like a coin nestled into the mouthpiece. About the size of a quarter.

"What's wrong?" said Rootie.

I put my hand over the phone.

"This phone is tapped," I said.

"What?" said Rootie. "It can't be." She jumped up and looked at the bug.

I put the phone down like it had a disease.

We both stared at the phone.

"I thought Farrell checked the whole place," said Rootie.

"I guess he missed one," I said.

"Now they know all about Cutlass and everything," said Rootie. "When we're going, how, where—the works."

I nodded. "The good part is now Farrell can probably trace it," I said. "They have equipment for that. He can find out who's after us."

"Call him tomorrow morning," said Rootie.

"I will," I said. "From a pay phone."

Mooshy never called back, and finally I went to bed.

It was hard to sleep that night. Somewhere, in between dreams, I got the idea that I would write a letter to my father.

He had written to me. I'd write him back. Then I'd leave it for him someplace on Cutlass Island.

Rootie says when people die, they're just plain dead, and that's that. But I think maybe they can sort of hear us if we're on the right kind of channel. It sounds wacky, but so what? A whole lot of things are strange, and we just ignore them if they don't happen to fit in with what we're used to. In the past, I had a feeling sometimes my mother—sick and crazy and locked away in that hospital—was still near me, and caring about me. I couldn't prove it, but that's what I felt.

And sometimes I thought about Biscuit, and she was so alive in my heart, so close, it was like she was there. I knew she would remember me, and all the time and distance melted away then, and it was as if she was lying next to me, with her velvety ears and her cold wet nose and her fur full of straw.

So around three in the morning, I turned on the light and wrote my father.

What I wrote was short—only a few sentences. *Dear Dad,* I wrote. *I got your letter. I know you loved me. I always knew that, no matter what. I loved you, too. You taught me about being strong. Now I'm trying to be strong, too, like you. Your son, Pete.*

Then I went to bed, and dreamed about treasure.

CHAPTER 15

The Unprotected Witness

In the morning, Mooshy still hadn't called, so we had missed the boat. We decided we had to put off the trip until the next morning. Rootie told her grandmother she would be going on a school outing the next day. Her class was going to take a bus up the Hudson River to Hyde Park, she said, where President Roosevelt had lived.

It seemed like a good choice by Rootie, as it turned out, because Mrs. Bowditch knew all about Hyde Park and President Roosevelt, and thought it was an excellent thing for the school to do.

I said I had permission to go, too, because my school thought it would be educational.

We would be leaving very early in the morning.

So much for the lies. But we passed through them

without any alarms going off, and then we were in the clear, and Mrs. Bowditch was putting marmalade on her toast and reminiscing about the old days up the Hudson.

"Not particularly lovely or old, Hyde Park," said Mrs. Bowditch. "I don't believe the Roosevelts were much for putting on the dog."

"Putting on the dog?" said Rootie.

"Showing off," said Mrs. Bowditch. "I suppose that's an obsolete term. I still like it. I'm obsolete myself. No idea where it came from." She began buttering another triangle of toast. "The Hudson River in those days was full of rather grand families, and they didn't necessarily get along with one another. Before he became crippled, young Franklin used to row on the river—he had one of those beautiful single sculls, you know?"

"No," I said.

"No," said Rootie.

"It's like an eight-man shell, made of that same thin, varnished, lovely wood? But it's for one person."

We nodded. I pictured eight men in a big wooden clamshell.

"In any case," she said, "there was a rivalry with the next great house along the river, and every year they held a race. If the neighbor didn't happen to have a son around to row, they'd just assign a chauffeur or a butler to do the rowing." She smiled. "You'll have a good time up there. They have the president's old open car—it's a beauty, with a running board and those big fenders. And his office—hard to believe he could run a country from that desk when he was up there."

I was beginning to think we should have said we were going to the Boston Museum or someplace. Mrs. Bowditch knew too much.

"By the time Mr. Roosevelt had been president for a while, most of those neighbors weren't speaking to him anymore. I doubt he cared. He saved the country, that's the main thing."

It was time for school.

I looked for Farrell's number in my wallet. No luck. In my backpack. Couldn't find it.

I looked in the Yellow Pages. They had the marshals listed under Law Enforcement. I wrote the number on my wrist with a ballpoint.

I said good-bye to Rootie and Mrs. Bowditch. There was a pay phone on Fifth Avenue. I decided to use that, even though the buses were grinding by and cars and trucks were honking their horns.

"United States marshals," said a woman's voice.

"Mr. Jack Farrell, please," I said.

"One moment, please," she said.

Long pause.

"We have no one by that name," she said.

"He's a United States marshal," I said. "Witness protection."

"I'm checking." Another pause. "I'm sorry," she said. "Nobody by that name works here."

"He *does* work there," I said. "Could I speak to one of the other marshals, please?"

"One moment."

The buses were making that loud whooshing sound. It was really hard to hear.

"Morgan here," said a distant voice on the phone.

"I'm trying to locate Jack Farrell," I shouted into the phone.

"There's no Farrell here," he said.

I was getting desperate. "He was assigned to do the follow-up on me after my father died in the witness protection program," I said.

"He told you that?" said the man.

"Yes!" I yelled. A bike rider swerved onto the sidewalk and around the phone.

"There's no follow-up," the man said. "When a witness dies, the case is closed."

"That can't be right," I shouted. A taxi driver was leaning on his horn: *Beeeeep. Beeeeeep.*

"You want me to say it again?" said the man.

"The case is closed?" I said. "That's it?"

"Now you got it, son," he said. "Who is this, anyway?"

I hung up.

All that day, while I walked around the city in a daze, up one street, down the other, the man's words rang in my head: "Now you got it, son."

What took me so long to get it? Why didn't I know it right away? There were plenty of hints and clues. But I had wanted to believe that Farrell was a good guy, a decent person, and that he would help save us. I wanted to believe that we had the entire official United States of America protecting us from the people who killed my father and Mr. Creech, and who would just as soon kill us, too, if we got in their way.

All it took Farrell was a phony little white card with an emblem on it, and a fake phone line, and I was totally fooled.

Because I wanted to be.

Now we were in real danger.

But at least I had an idea who the enemy was. A nice friendly guy with a big grin and a helpful manner. A regular person. Smooth. Made you feel confidence in him.

Whatever it was my father had buried on Cutlass Island, they wanted that, and they were going to get it.

Unless we got it first.

And then what? Then they would get *us*.

Rootie and I were the last targets.

I was an unprotected witness. So was Rootie. We were the unprotected witnesses.

"Now you got it, son," said the voice.

When Rootie got back from school, I told her about Farrell.

"Bastard!" she said. "What a slimy bastard."

"Did you ever trust him in the first place?" I said.

"Yes, I think I did," said Rootie.

"Me, too," I said.

Later that night, Rootie said to me, "Why don't we leave the tap in the phone?"

"Why?" I said.

"Then we can pretend we didn't find it. We can make Farrell think anything we want him to think."

"Good idea," I said. "We'll call Mooshy and tell him the trip to Cutlass was just a joke."

"Then we can take the bug out of the phone, and call him back and arrange the trip."

"Very smart," I said.

Finally, around ten o'clock, Mooshy called. "Greetings, one and all," he said. "Moosh Limo is at your service."

"Where have you been, Moosh?" I said. "We've been trying to reach you."

"I had to go someplace," he said. "I'll tell you another time. Hey, are we going to Cutlass Island?"

"Oh, no, man," I said, trying to sound surprised. "That was just a gag. Did you believe it? Sorry, man. Rootie and I were just kidding. There isn't any treasure."

"Oh," said Mooshy. "I see." He didn't exactly sound as if he understood.

"Well, it's kind of late, Mooshman. I've got a test tomorrow in school, so I better hit the sack."

"Okay, Pete," said Mooshy. "Talk to you tomorrow."

I hung up. "How was that?" I asked Rootie.

"Cool," she said.

"Do you think Farrell fell for it?"

"Maybe," said Rootie.

I took the bug out of the phone and called Mooshy back.

"Moosh," I said. "There was a bug in the phone just now when I was talking to you. So disregard everything I said, okay? Now I've taken the bug out. Here's the real story. Farrell planted the bug. He's not a witness-protection agent at all. He's a mob guy. Our trip to Cutlass Island is definitely on for tomorrow morning, if you can make it. There's a treasure buried out there—my father wrote me a letter about it."

"Slow down, man," said Mooshy. "Can we review some of the material here?"

"Sorry, Moosh," I said. "I guess I was going fast." I went over it again, until Mooshy got the full picture. "What do you think, Moosh—do you want to go?"

"Do bears crap in the woods?" said Mooshy. "Absolutely I want to go."

"Where's your car?"

"At 104th and Second," he said. "Or maybe 106th."

"We'll meet you," I said.

"Six A.M.?"

"You got it, Moosh. You're a pal." I hung up. "All set," I said to Rootie.

We went up onto the roof and sat around for a while,

trying to calm down. The roof had seemed like a safe place once, but now we were suspicious of everything, and we sort of whispered when we talked. I looked at the big buildings around us, the lighted windows in the dark, and now they seemed like the eyes of rats, like the ones in that empty lot in the Bronx. They were watching, waiting to move.

Suddenly I was scared.

"Rootie," I said. "What would you think if . . . if we got ourselves out of this whole thing. You know, just dumped it. Let them have whatever's buried on the island."

Rootie stared at me. "You mean chicken out?"

"I mean stay alive. Not die because of some crazy thing my father did."

Rootie didn't say anything for a minute. Then she said, "You know what? You're probably right. We should get out of this as fast as we can. We'd be really dumb to go running up to Cutlass when we know they'll follow us and probably try to kill us."

"It would be asking for it," I said.

"It would be a stupid thing to do," said Rootie.

Just then we heard the phone ringing downstairs. Rootie went down the ladder first, then down the stairs. By the time I got there, she was hanging up.

"That was Moosh," she said.

"What happened?" I said.

"He was calling from a pay phone in the street."

"Why?"

"He decided to check out the phone in his apartment."

"And?"

"It was bugged," she said. "Just like ours."

C H A P T E R 16

The Blue Beauty

Next morning at six A.M. Rootie and I had to hunt around 104th Street for the blue Lincoln. It wasn't exactly where Mooshy had said it would be, and rain was coming down sideways in the dark, hitting us in the face. We stood in the doorway of a convenience store for a while, looking out at the dark street through streams of water.

"This is a big mistake," I said.

"Chill out," said Rootie. "We'll be okay. Farrell won't do anything until we actually have the treasure in our hands."

"Maybe we should have waited a week or two," I said.

"What good would that do?" said Rootie. "They'd still come after us."

"I guess you're right," I said.

"Let's find the money, okay?" said Rootie. "Then we'll deal with the next step. Maybe we'll be calling the cops."

Rootie went into the store and bought some doughnuts while I watched for Mooshy—or Farrell.

Rootie came out and gave me a doughnut. It tasted great. I felt better right away, and then Mooshy was coming down the street, calling to us.

"Come on," he yelled. "The blue beauty awaits!"

The Lincoln convertible was partway down the block. There was a small lake on the car's roof where the old canvas sagged, and a fistful of soggy parking tickets were stuffed under a windshield wiper.

Mooshy grabbed the front door on the driver's side with both hands. He put one foot up against the side of the car and pulled as hard as he could. The door slowly screeched open.

"Touch of rust," said Mooshy.

"You don't lock your car?" said Rootie.

"Who would take it?" said Mooshy.

Mooshy squatted down and reached under the steering wheel.

"What are you doing?" I asked.

"Hot-wiring the ignition," he said. "I lost the keys a

couple months back." He got in, and the car started making that groaning can't-start sound: aw-*oh.* Aw-*ohh.* Aw-*ohhh.* Finally, the engine gave a cough that shook the whole car. Mooshy gunned it a couple of times, and thick smoke poured out of the exhaust.

Mooshy climbed out of the car and went around the back. He crouched by the rear wheel and stuck his hand into the well.

"Got a flat?" said Rootie.

"No," said Mooshy. "Looking for something."

He got up and checked the other wheel.

"Aha!" said Mooshy. "Gotcha!"

"What is it?" I said.

"Here comes a cop," said Rootie.

A police car was coming slowly up the avenue, the reflection of its red lights wobbling on the wet street.

"Start walking," said Mooshy. "Be casual."

We walked down the sidewalk, talking to one another, talking junk, any words at all—but really watching out of the corner of our eyes as the cruiser got closer.

"Going to Kansas City," said Rootie. "Kansas City, here I come."

"Return videos by three P.M.," said Mooshy.

The police car stopped ten yards ahead of us. The cop got out and looked at us.

"Serpentine, Shel." said Mooshy. "Serpentine." That was a line from an old movie where Peter Falk and Alan Arkin were dodging bullets.

Then the cop walked around his car and into the convenience store.

"Whew," said Rootie.

"What did you find, Mooshy?" I said.

Mooshy showed us a small black box. "It's a Lo-Jack," he said. "Your friend Farrell must have stuck it under the fender."

"What does it do?" said Rootie.

"It attaches to your car by magnet," said Mooshy, "and it sends out a powerful signal. If somebody has the right equipment, they can find your car and follow it wherever it goes."

"Somebody knows where it is right this minute?" said Rootie.

"I figure," said Mooshy.

"They could follow us to the boat?"

"Sure," said Mooshy. "And it has a range of several miles. You'd never see them."

So that's why Farrell wasn't around, I thought. He doesn't need to be. He's just waiting for us to go.

"Well, you better throw that thing away," said Rootie.

"I got a better idea," said Mooshy. He walked over to the police car. He gave a quick glance toward the convenience store, then he ducked down and stuck his arm into the rear-wheel well.

"I can't believe this," said Rootie. "That Mooshy guy has major balls."

Mooshy came strolling back down the sidewalk. He had a big grin on his face. "I've bought us a little extra time," he said. "Your friend will probably follow that signal around New York all morning—at least until he discovers it's on a police car."

"Brilliant," said Rootie. "Definitely brilliant." Her attitude toward Mooshy was changing fast.

"Good move, Moosh," I said.

"All aboard, everybody," said Mooshy.

Rootie climbed into the back, and I sat in the passenger seat. The interior of the car was full of gray duct tape. The tape held together the gearshift, the handle on the window, the rearview mirror. It kept the glove compartment closed and the stuffing in the front seat. The roof was crisscrossed with it. Loose ends of tape dangled down like vines in a jungle.

"Keep your feet off the metal there, Rootie," said Mooshy. "The rug wore away, and it gets really hot from the exhaust pipe." Rootie put her feet up on the seat.

"There's a leak in the roof," she said, wiping her neck.

"I'm putting it at the top of my list," said Mooshy.

He gunned the engine. One wheel of the car went up on the sidewalk, than banged down onto the street, and we were on our way.

"How are those windshield wipers, Mooshy?" called Rootie. "Do you think you should turn them on, seeing as how we're in a downpour?"

"Good idea," said Mooshy. He turned on the wipers. The traffic tickets went flying. "Much better visibility," said Mooshy. "Thanks, Rootie."

"How about headlights?" I said. "It's kind of dark out there."

"Wish I could, Pete," said Mooshy, "but you know, a car this age, there's bound to be some part that doesn't work."

"The headlights don't work?" I said.

"Not on a regular basis," said Mooshy. "That's why I prefer to drive in the daytime."

We went rattling along for a while. Then suddenly I remembered. "Hold it!" I said. "I forgot something."

"What's the matter?" said Mooshy.

"We have to go back to the house," I said.

"We'll miss the boat," said Rootie.

"It won't take a minute," I said.

"Is it really important?" said Rootie.

"Yes," I said. It was the letter to my father.

Ten minutes later we turned into 64th Street. Halfway down the block I saw Farrell's red Geo Prizm. It was parked a few houses down from Rootie's place.

"Stop!" I said to Mooshy. "That's Farrell!"

Mooshy hit the brakes.

I was glad we didn't have the headlights then. Mooshy slid the car over to the curb and parked. We watched through the rain what happened next.

Farrell got out and called across the top of the car to somebody who was standing in a doorway. He waved impatiently, like "Come on! Come on!"

Then, from the doorway, a man in a hat and raincoat

came running across the sidewalk toward the car. He jumped in.

It was Big Mac.

"They're in it together," I said to Rootie. "Big Mac and Farrell."

Then Little Hot Dog was running after him, his short legs moving as fast as they could, and his leash dragging behind him on the sidewalk.

As Hot Dog reached the open door of the car, Big Mac stuck out his foot and shoved the dog in the chest, hard. Hot Dog fell backward, his feet scrambling in the air. The car door slammed, and the red car sprayed a wall of water as it took off down the street. A few seconds later, it was gone.

"Oh, my god," said Rootie.

We pulled up to the house. Hot Dog was yelping, running back and forth, back and forth, stopping to look at where the car had gone, then running again.

Rootie was out of the car like a shot. She ran over to the little dog and crouched down beside it.

I went into the house and got my letter from my room. Then I ran down the stairs and out to the car. I jumped in, and Mooshy hit the gas. In the backseat, Rootie was holding Hot Dog in her arms, crooning to him, smoothing his wet fur, trying to calm him down. The little dog was shaking all over and whimpering.

"Rootie," I said. "Where are you taking the dog?"

"Cutlass Island," she said. "He's my dog now."

CHAPTER 17

Cutlass Island

By 6:45 we were across the Triboro Bridge, leaving the toll collector in a cloud of blue exhaust. Mooshy drove with his nose hardly higher than the dashboard. He kept up a conversation with the other cars: "Look out, buster—the Connie is coming through," "Hello, grampa—stick to your lane now," "Whoa, that was a close one."

I told Rootie to watch out the back for the red Geo.

"Anybody care for a marshmallow?" said Mooshy.

"Marshmallows?" said Rootie.

"In the glove compartment," said Mooshy.

I peeled off some duct tape and took out a battered box. There were half a dozen marshmallows in it, like somebody's rock collection.

"Put a few of those babies on the floor back there, Rootie," said Mooshy.

"Are you kidding?" said Rootie.

"Don't you want 'em toasted?" said Mooshy.

Rootie dropped a handful on the metal floor. Pretty soon they were turning brown.

"Want one?" said Rootie.

"Sure," I said. "Not too well done, please."

"There's a screwdriver under the seat," said Mooshy. "You can use that for a fork."

She found the screwdriver and stabbed a marshmallow for me.

"Pretty good, Mooshy," I said, "except for the taste of motor oil."

"Tell your complaints to the head waiter," said Mooshy. "Give me a burnt one, Rootie."

She dug a crusty black one off the floor. It pulled apart. Finally she just handed Mooshy the screwdriver with the marshmallow on it.

"Delicious," said Mooshy.

"The floor back here is a sticky mess," said Rootie.

"That's the trouble with marshmallows," said Mooshy. "Usually I just fry eggs, and maybe some bacon."

Rootie made a retching noise.

After an hour or so, we spotted a McDonald's. Mooshy went skidding sideways into a parking spot.

Mooshy had two sausage biscuits and an order of hash browns. Rootie and I weren't too hungry after the marshmallows. Rootie got a plain sausage biscuit to go, for Hot Dog, and a cup of water. Hot Dog wouldn't touch the sausage. He just smelled it and turned away.

"Tells you something, doesn't it?" said Rootie. Hot Dog lapped up some water, and we hit the road again.

Still no red car.

After a couple of hours, there were no more cities. The land flattened out and turned sandy, and forests of low pine trees lined the road. Every so often we would pass a gas station, but that was about it. You could get a glimpse of the ocean sometimes, and maybe a hawk floating overhead. The rain had stopped, but it was still a gray, windy day.

"Can I hold Hot Dog for a little while?" I said.

"Sure," said Rootie. She handed him over the seat.

For the next hour, Hot Dog slept in my arms, and it was great. It made me think of those summer afternoons in Oklahoma with Biscuit. I guess I fell asleep, too, because next thing I knew we were coming down the road to Port of Hope.

"This is my kind of town," said Mooshy when we drove into Port of Hope. On both sides of the street were video arcades, salt water taffy and ice-cream shops, bars, bike and moped rental places, T-shirt and souvenir stores, clam bars, and parking lots with guys standing in the street, trying to wave cars in. "Plenty to do around here," he said. Then he stopped the car. "I have to tell you something," he said.

"What's the matter, Moosh?" I said.

"I'm scared of boats, and I get really seasick. I don't think I can go on that ferry."

"That's okay, Moosh," I said.

"Is it all right if I hang out," he said, "and meet you when you get back?"

Rootie said that was fine.

We pulled up to the ferry and got out.

"Thanks for the ride, Moosh," I said. "We'll meet you here at two o'clock when the noon boat comes back from the island."

"What if you're not on it?" said Moosh.

"We'll be on it," said Moosh.

"What about Hot Dog?" I said. "Maybe Mooshy should take her while we're on the island?"

"You want to?" Rootie asked Mooshy.

"I can't," said Mooshy. "They won't allow dogs in the places I'm going. Like arcades and stuff."

"We'll take Hot Dog," said Rootie. "It'll be okay."

"Thanks," said Mooshy. "Good luck out there."

"You're a pal," said Rootie. "Thanks."

Mooshy drove off.

Rootie and Hot Dog and I stood in line for tickets to the boat. It was a small ferry—room for maybe fifteen cars, and only one passenger deck with the cabin above that. The flags were flying straight out. It could be a rough trip on the small boat.

I kept looking around, checking the passengers. No Big Mac or Farrell—just people with bags of groceries, backpacks, cameras, and weekend stuff. Babies in strollers, dogs on leashes, kids running around.

We got our tickets and went aboard. Rootie picked up Hot Dog and carried him up the outside stairs to the passenger deck above the cars. The cabin was small and already full—some people were lying down on the long white box of life preservers—so we stood outside by the rail, looking at the docks and fishing boats of Port of Hope.

Black metal masts stuck up from the fishing boats—cranes and cables and ladders and lines and pulleys jumbled together—it looked like a construction site in the city. Colored nets were wrapped around huge drums on the sterns.

Rootie took a deep breath. "Ah," she said. "Good old Port of Hope perfume."

It came from all around us—from the open hold of the rusty green fishing boat at the next dock, where men in oilskins were standing knee-deep in fish, shoveling them into a big bucket swinging over their heads. It came from the dock beyond, where a bunch of workers with pitchforks were stabbing what looked like skates and other creatures and stuffing them into rows of blue barrels. It came from the white mountains of clam shells behind the nearest clam bar, and the overloaded Dumpsters and garbage cans, and it all blended with the aroma of rancid cooking oil and fried onions. Some passengers turned green before they were even on the boat.

The ship's horn gave a blast that made us jump, and the ship rumbled out into the river and turned toward the sea. I looked back at the dock to see if Farrell or Big Mac was there, but it was all clear.

We didn't hit any waves until we passed the breakwater. Then a big lazy roller passed under us, shivering the boat, and dropped us in its wake. I fell back across the deck and grabbed the wheel on one of the fire hoses that were mounted on the bulkhead. Hot Dog jumped out of Rootie's arms and dived under a bench. He never moved from that spot till we tied up at Cutlass Island an hour later.

For part of the trip, Rootie and I sat on the bench above Hot Dog, sort of sheltering him with our legs, but when the waves got too enormous, we had to stand up and hold on to one of the poles of the railing with both hands. The waves came at the boat in walls of water—nearly vertical, topped with foaming whitecaps—and slammed into the side, throwing water across the deck, through the open mesh of the railings. Hot Dog scrunched down as the water sloshed against him. The boat shuddered, and fell, and rose again. We hung on to the pole as tightly as we could.

Rootie shouted something I couldn't hear, even though her face was only a couple of feet away.

"What?" I yelled. The wind ripped the word out of my mouth and carried it away.

"I'm glad Mooshy isn't here!" she yelled, and laughed.

That was Rootie—hanging on for dear life in the middle of a wild ocean—and laughing.

I couldn't even smile. To me, we were on a dark, dangerous roller coaster. No colored lights, no tinny music, no squealing people.

A man in an orange parka came running out of the cabin, threw himself against the railing, and vomited.

"Duck!" yelled Rootie to me, and we both turned our heads away. But the wind must have been right—we were okay. Then we watched the poor guy lurching back across the slippery deck, trying to reach the cabin, dancing a strange dance with his arms waving—two steps this way, kick, two steps back, kick, one step forward, and slide. By the time he finally dove through the door of the cabin, I was laughing, too.

When we landed on Cutlass Island, the boat screeching against the pilings, Rootie and I didn't waste any time. We led Hot Dog through an alley between the stores and hotels and went straight for Rootie's old shortcut—the Yellow Brick Road was what she named it—that went up through the woods to the road next to my house. The path was still muddy in places, and full of rocks and moss and ferns and bullbriar and blackberry bushes and skunk cabbage. You could see traces of the bicycle tracks Rootie and I had left in the summer, when we used the road all the time. But now the leaves overhead were changing, and instead of green it was like going through a tunnel of yellow and red and brown. The wind wailed above us, but it was calm below.

The house that my father and I lived in looked exactly the same, except for a FOR RENT sign on the front lawn. There, next to the porch, was the window where my father sat each day, the gun at his right hand and the glass of vodka in his left, watching the road for the man who would come to kill him.

Rootie and I ran across the lawn to the back of the house with Hot Dog following us. At the edge of the woods, we could see the big tree, and through the thinning leaves, high up, the edge of the tree house we had built together.

"Let's climb up and take a look," I said to Rootie.

"Hey, we're in a hurry, remember?" said Rootie.

I could see where one of the steps was missing—the step that broke when Looney Tunes was standing on it. And there ahead of us was the flat rock that killed him when he fell. "Where's a shovel?" said Rootie.

"Probably in the cellar," I said. I ran back to the house. The outside door to the cellar was halfway off its hinges. I remembered how Looney Tunes came barreling down the stairs and chased me, shooting. I was down there hunting for the gun I had hidden from my father. That was in the days when I worried my father was going to shoot himself.

I pulled open the broken door. There was a shovel leaning against the cellar wall, next to some rakes. I grabbed it and ran back to where Rootie was standing by the rock.

"I've been looking at the ground here," she said, pointing. "There's a little area where nothing much is growing. It might be a good place to start."

I looked back at the road to make sure nobody was there. Then I stuck the shovel in the ground and began to dig. Sometimes I hit the edge of the rock with a clang, but the earth was soft, and in a few minutes—*thud*—I hit something else.

It was the top of a suitcase. One of those old-fashioned leather suitcases. Brown. Rootie crouched down and started to scoop dirt away with her hands. "Hey," she said. "There are two suitcases here."

I kneeled down and began digging with my bare hands, too.

In a couple of minutes, we were able to grab the handle and haul the first suitcase out of the ground. It was worn and moldy, and it weighed a lot.

"We have to look inside," said Rootie.

The suitcase had a lock in the middle and clasps on either side.

"How are we going to unlock it?" I said.

"Maybe we smash the lock with a sledgehammer or something?" said Rootie.

"Then we couldn't close it again to carry it," I said.

"What if we got a crowbar and pried it open?"

"I don't know if there is one here," I said. "I'll go look in the cellar. Maybe there's a big branch cutter or something."

I started for the cellar.

"Wait a minute," said Rootie. "Hold everything!"

Before I could turn around, a bunch of money whirled past me, like butterflies carried by the wind. I looked back. Rootie was in the middle of a tornado of bills flying up from the open suitcase.

"Guess what!" yelled Rootie. "It wasn't locked!" With one hand, she was trying to snatch the money as it went by; with the other hand, she was trying to close the suitcase.

"Kneel on it!" I shouted. "The money's going everywhere!" The bills were sailing into the trees, catching on the branches, darting across the grass toward the road.

I stepped on a bill, and then picked it up. One hundred dollars.

Then I was running all over the yard, Hot Dog chasing

me, snagging the bills as fast as I could. They kept soaring out of my reach. Rootie yelled that she'd gotten the suitcase closed, and then both of us were racing around, scooping up money, jumping in the air for it, stuffing our pockets with wads. The air was full of it, and Rootie and I were like little kids let out to play in the first big snow.

CHAPTER 18

Overboard

The other suitcase was locked, and maybe twice as heavy as the first one. I couldn't budge it. Rootie tried to help me. We both pulled as hard as we could—and the handle snapped off.

"What do we do now?" I said.

"Leave it," said Rootie.

"But it's full of money," I said.

"Then pick it up and carry it yourself," she said.

"We'll bury it," I said. "Then we'll come back later."

While Rootie was gathering up hundred-dollar bills from around the house and the road, I tore the letter to my father into a lot of little pieces and dropped them in the hole next to the heavy suitcase. Then I filled the hole with dirt. It wasn't the best place in the world to leave my letter—if I had a choice, I probably would have floated it into the rapids back at Collyer's Spring—but at least it was done and over, and I stamped the earth down with my foot and spread a bunch of leaves over the dirt.

Rootie tied a piece of clothesline around the other suitcase so it wouldn't fall open.

"I'll carry it first," she said. "When it gets too heavy, I'll give it to you."

"Okay," I said. I put Hot Dog on his leash. I took one last look at the tree house, and we started toward the road.

"I better make sure nobody's coming," I said. "Then we'll cross the road fast."

Rootie waited while I put the shovel back in the cellar. Then I looked around the side of the house. The road was empty. "Let's go," I said.

We were halfway across when we heard a car coming. Rootie ran to the other side and climbed over the wall, lugging the suitcase, and disappeared into the woods.

I tried to follow her, but Hot Dog stopped in the road, looking toward the sound. "Come *on*, Hot Dog," I said. "Come on!" I pulled at his leash.

But Hot Dog wouldn't move. The car came up the

hill. I couldn't see who was in it. When the car got close, it began to slow down.

I didn't know what to do. I decided to pick up Hot Dog and climb over the wall.

I gave his leash a yank.

His collar slipped off over his head.

Now I was standing in the road holding the leash with the collar at one end, dangling, and Hot Dog was alone.

"Hot Dog, come here!" I said. Hot Dog didn't budge.

The car was coming to a stop.

Should I climb over the wall and just leave Hot Dog behind?

The car stopped. Hot Dog began barking at it. I couldn't see who was in the car—it looked like two people. The front door opened on the driver's side.

I could hear Rootie calling me from the woods. "Run, Pete! Run!"

But I couldn't leave Hot Dog.

Then the front door closed again. On the side of the car I saw a sign: ISLAND REAL ESTATE, it said.

The car started up and drove away.

I guess whoever it was didn't like the looks of the house.

I slipped the collar back on Hot Dog, and we went over the wall and into the woods where Rootie was waiting.

We sneaked off through the town, keeping our eyes open, and then hid behind the freight building at the dock. Rootie peeked out at the boat.

"See anybody?" I said.

"No," said Rootie. "Not many people going aboard, either."

I took a look.

It was one of the big white ferries—the kind with three passenger decks above the car deck—sort of like an old Mississippi steamboat. They were better in a rough sea than the small ferries. But not much. The big boat pulled at its lines and the pilings creaked.

"Those guys could be waiting for us," I said. "Somewhere on this boat." I looked at the decks overhead.

"We'll check it out," said Rootie. "Come on."

We went aboard, up the stairs, and into the big cabin on the first passenger deck. There was an old woman at one of the tables. She had some plastic bags, and she was reading the newspaper. A few tables away were three young guys in fancy bicycling clothes. They were laughing and hooting. Across the deck was a businessman with papers and a laptop. He wasn't wasting a minute. An elderly couple with a Pekingese settled down at a table. They wrapped the dog's leash around a leg of a bench. The dog saw Hot Dog and started barking, so we went to the other side of the ship. A bearded guy was sitting with a knapsack, his hands folded, staring straight ahead. Near him, a couple of men in parkas were sharing a big map, pointing to things. Real-estate developers, maybe—figuring what they could do to Cutlass.

We went up the stairs to the second deck. This one had an outside deck around the cabin, and inside there were long blue benches facing inward. Nobody was in the cabin, or even on the deck as far as we could tell.

"Maybe we should settle here," I said.

"Too dangerous," said Rootie. "We'd be all alone up here if something happened."

"Let's go back to the first deck," I said, "where there's people. Farrell wouldn't do anything in front of people, would he?"

"I don't know," said Rootie. We went back down the stairs and sat next to one of the windows. The gulls were gliding by, getting free rides on the wind.

I went outside on the stern and watched the dock. I didn't see anything special. A surfer arrived, limping, carrying his board, and one couple on a motorcycle. That was it.

The horn went off. I went back in. "So far, so good," I said. I didn't really mean it. I guess it was like crossing my fingers.

The ship began to move.

"They could still be on board somewhere," said Rootie. "Keep your eyes open."

Hot Dog lay down under the table next to the suitcase, his long ears stretched out on the deck, and went to sleep.

"What if they come after us?" I said. "What's the plan?"

"Plan?" said Rootie. "You *wish* we had a plan!" She laughed. "All we can do is run, and maybe hide."

"Should we stick together, or separate, or what?"

"It's the suitcase they want," said Rootie. "Whoever has the suitcase . . ." Her voice trailed off.

"Maybe we should hide now," I said. "There's a lot of places, Down where the cars are, behind the life rafts, inside a lifeboat, in the men's or ladies' room on the top deck, up by the pilot house. We could hide now."

"How do you know that Farrell and Big Mac aren't hiding in those places right this minute—just waiting?" said Rootie.

I didn't have an answer to that.

Now I was more scared than before. The waves were shoving the boat around now. I held on to the edge of the table. Suddenly Rootie said, "Where's Hot Dog?" I looked under the table. He was gone. We grabbed the suitcase and went to find him. He wasn't anywhere around. We looked all over the deck.

"You look in the men's room," said Rootie. "I'll wait here."

I looked into the men's room.

Hot Dog was standing just inside the open door, looking toward one of the stalls and growling. The stall was occupied. The door was closed. A man with big feet—black shoes and dark pants—was sitting in there.

I knew it was Big Mac. Hot Dog knew it, too. Big Mac was hiding. Just sitting there, using the toilet as a place to wait.

I grabbed Hot Dog and ran back to Rootie. I told her what I'd seen, and we went out onto the stern of the ferry and crouched down behind one of the big wooden boxes of life jackets.

"We know where Big Mac is," said Rootie. "But where's Farrell?"

We stayed there, hunched down, Rootie hugging Hot Dog, for maybe twenty minutes.

"I have an idea," said Rootie. "What if we go up to the pilot house? We can tell the captain what's happening—"

"What can *he* do?"

"I don't know, but maybe something. At least we won't be sitting here like a target."

"Let's go," I said.

We started up the outside stairs to the next deck. Near the top, Rootie stopped. "They're here," she said.

We ducked down and looked over the top step.

Farrell and Big Mac were standing by the rail, twenty yards away. Even though you couldn't hear anything because of the wind, you could tell they were having an argument. They shouted, they pointed at each other, they shook their fists. Big Mac grabbed Farrell by the lapels of his coat, and Farrell knocked his hands away. He gave Big Mac a shove. Their faces were only a few inches apart, yelling, and then Farrell suddenly whirled away and marched off. Big Mac shouted something in

Farrell's direction, then turned back to the sea. He straightened his coat with a shake, as if he were saying, I guess I told *him*.

"We better hide," said Rootie.

"Farrell's going to find—"

Rootie never finished what she was saying.

At that moment, Farrell came back from behind the cabin. He came at a dead run, charging like a bull toward Big Mac. He raised one arm in the air. Big Mac never saw it coming, and when Farrell delivered a savage chop with the side of his hand to Big Mac's neck, the heavy man went limp. Then Farrell was tackling him around the knees with both arms, lifting, heaving him upward.

"He's not going to do it," said Rootie. "Is he?"

You could see how heavy Big Mac was, and how hard it was to get him off the deck, even though his arms were limp and he wasn't even trying to grab the rail.

But then, suddenly, it was easy, because now Farrell had Big Mac more than halfway over the side. Farrell only had to let go.

He let go.

Big Mac slipped over the rail as easily as a sea lion sliding off its rock in the Central Park Zoo.

Farrell stared over the railing. His head turned slowly toward the ship's wake, watching.

Hot Dog began to bark.

Rootie tried to stop him, but it was too late. Farrell's head snapped around toward the sound, and he saw us, frozen there, our heads sticking up above the top step of the stairs, and then he was coming toward us.

Hot Dog jumped out of Rootie's arms and tried to run down the metal steps. Rootie went after him, and I ran behind Rootie. I thought we could make it because we were almost down to the bottom of the stairs. But I got one foot tangled in Hot Dog's leash, and I stumbled and fell down on the deck, knocking Rootie over as I went.

By the time we looked up, Farrell was jumping down the stairs, three or four steps at a time.

Rootie got up and grabbed the suitcase.

"Give me that suitcase," said Farrell.

"No," said Rootie.

"Give it to him, Rootie," I said. "It's okay."

With a sudden lunge, Farrell snatched Hot Dog off the deck and took him to the railing.

"Put him down!" screamed Rootie.

"Where?" said Farrell. He grabbed Hot Dog by his

long ears, holding them in his fist. "Here?" he said, dangling the dog over the deck. "Or here?" He swung Hot Dog over the ocean, letting him swing slowly back and forth. Hot Dog was looking at us: Why don't you help me?

"Give me my dog," shouted Rootie. "You can have the damn money!" She slammed the suitcase on the deck.

Farrell grinned. He swung Hot Dog in a slow, lazy circle. Hot Dog's paws were digging at the air.

"Get up on the railing, both of you," he said.

Rootie and I just stood there. I couldn't move.

"Get up!" Farrell yelled.

"Give me my dog," said Rootie. "First." The tears were streaming down her face.

"When you get on the railing," said Farrell. He reached for the suitcase, still holding Hot Dog over the water.

I went to the railing first.

Farrell said, "Climb up."

I grabbed a pole and started to climb up onto the rail. The sea was heaving below me. I had one leg up when I heard the noise behind me.

Farrell heard it, too, and swung around. The instant Hot Dog swung over the deck again, Rootie gave Farrell a terrific kick. Farrell howled and doubled over. Hot Dog fell onto the deck and ran. By the time Farrell stood up again, and looked toward the noise—the sudden, high-pitched noise—it was too late for him.

Maybe if he had let go of the suitcase, he could have grabbed hold of the railing with both hands. But that wouldn't have helped for long. Maybe a few seconds. Not long.

All he could do, really, was watch as the water from the fire hose came at him, roaring, and lifted him off his feet, pushing him against the rail as Mooshy, his glasses gleaming under his hood, played the blast of water over him like a fireman putting out a fire. Mooshy could barely hang on to the canvas hose, but he planted his feet and kept the nozzle pointed straight at Farrell's body.

Farrell was holding the suitcase in both arms now, clutching it to his chest like a life preserver as the water carried him into the air and away from the boat. He hung in the air for a minute, the water spraying off him, and then he went straight down, his coat flying up like an inside-out umbrella, and he was gone.

Mooshy let go of the hose, and it took off on its own, snaking down the deck, spraying in all directions.

Mooshy staggered to the rail and threw up.

Rootie was next. She ran to the rail, and then it was suddenly my turn. All three of us were lined up on the rail, hanging on for dear life, sick and green and miserable. Behind us, Hot Dog barked and barked as the boat pushed on through the steep waves.

CHAPTER 19

The Conga

They never found Farrell or Big Mac, and after a while the Coast Guard gave up looking. An officer named Grady told us that with the sea running high and the direction of the wind and tide, the men had probably been carried out into the Atlantic.

I don't know about the suitcase. I guess Farrell finally let go of it. Or maybe that was what pulled him under. Maybe he couldn't let go.

Later on, Mooshy told us how he had wandered around Port of Hope that morning, and when he saw Farrell and Big Mac get on the boat, he decided he'd better get aboard, too. So he sneaked down to where the cars were parked and hid in the back of a truck for a while, getting sicker and sicker.

"Farrell and Big Mac didn't even get off the boat at

Cutlass," he said. "They just waited for you two to get on board. So I waited, too. When the boat was out in the ocean, I came up from below where I was hiding, and there was Farrell holding Hot Dog over the side. I looked around for a weapon. I saw a fire ax on the wall, but I didn't think I could do much with that. Then I saw the big canvas fire hose folded up there, and I decided to give it a try. I turned the wheel and the water came out fast, so I just went after Farrell with it."

"Thanks, Moosh," said Rootie. "You saved our lives."

"That's okay," said Mooshy. "But I'm never going on one of *those* boats again."

In the weeks after that, Mrs. Bowditch got a hotshot old lawyer, and Mooshy and Rootie and I were cleared. Self-defense. The lawyer told the newspapers and TV people about how a lot of the money—the three million dollars of drug money that my father had been supposed to deliver—had sunk to the bottom of the ocean and the rest had been found buried in a backyard on Cutlass Island. That made us feel free of the whole thing at last. Our connection was broken. No more running, no more being hunted, no more being chased down, no more fear.

There were rumors that people on Cutlass Island were

finding some of the money that had flown out of the suitcase when Rootie had opened it under the tree house. A kid would find a bill stuck in some tall grass at the edge of a field, or a farmer would see one jammed in the crack of a stone wall, or somebody walking on the beach would discover one tucked into a snow fence along the dunes.

Rootie and I both gave away most of the money we had stuffed in our pockets that day. I gave mine to Mooshy so he could make some improvements on the Lincoln—such as a floor and a roof, and maybe some new duct tape.

Rootie gave hers to a charity in New York that tries to help kids before it's too late—maybe kids like Farrell was once, and Big Mac, and my father, too.

In New York, things got better. Rootie and I started being close again, like the old days, and Mooshy was part of the whole deal.

One day he told Rootie and me where he had been that time when we couldn't reach him on the phone. He had gone out to Long Island to the cemetery where his brother was buried. It was a trip he took every year on the day his brother had died. Mooshy didn't tell anybody, and nobody else was ever there. The cemetery was a small one out in the country. Mooshy took a sleeping bag and spent the night under a tree near the gravestone. Then, next day, he came back.

In the middle of everything was Hot Dog, of course. He ran up and down the stairs of the house like an Olympic hurdler, and Mrs. Bowditch really liked him. She was the one who gave him his new name.

"I don't think 'Hot Dog' befits his dignity," she said the first week. "He's a brave fellow, and he deserves a proper name."

"How about Frankfurter?" said Rootie.

"Better," said Mrs. Bowditch. "A lot better, but . . ."

"How about Frank or Franklin?" I said.

"Franklin is good," said Rootie. "What do you think, Grandma?"

"Excellent," said Mrs. Bowditch. "Like Franklin Roosevelt. Strong, courageous. I like it very much." She smiled. "Besides, if you two hadn't gone up to visit Franklin Roosevelt's house at Hyde Park that day, this splendid dog wouldn't be here."

"Did we fool you, Grandma?" said Rootie.

"You'll never know, will you?" said Mrs. Bowditch, smiling.

"That's true," said Rootie. "Franklin—you want a dog

biscuit?" She went to get him one, and he ran after her, his tail wagging.

One night in late November, Mrs. Bowditch told us she was not going to Cutlass Island the next summer. "I think we could all use a change, don't you?" she said.

"It depends," said Rootie. "What are we going to do instead?"

"Well," said Mrs. Bowditch. "Next June is my sixtieth reunion at Bryn Mawr. I intend to go and see who might possibly still be alive from our class."

"You be careful, Grandma," said Rootie. "You remember what happened to you at your fiftieth reunion."

"What happened?" I asked.

"She broke her hip doing the tango," said Rootie.

"That's not correct," said Mrs. Bowditch.

"What's not correct about it?" said Rootie. "You were in a cast for weeks."

"It was not the tango," said Mrs. Bowditch. "It was the conga."

"What's the difference?" said Rootie.

"The tango is danced by two people," said Mrs. Bowditch. "A conga is done by a long line of people, sometimes hundreds, one in front of the other, winding around all over the place."

"How does it go?" I said.

Mrs. Bowditch looked at me. "Do you really want to know?"

I nodded.

Mrs. Bowditch got slowly to her feet.

"Watch out, Grandma," said Rootie.

Mrs. Bowditch said, "One-two-three—kick! One-two-three—kick!" She swayed to the rhythm, then she stepped out, one step for each number, and then she kicked one leg across the other on the word "Kick!" She went carefully around the coffee table a couple of times, one-two-three-kicking, and then said, "Come along, Root—get behind me, and hold on!"

Rootie shot me a what-are-ya-gonna-do? look and shrugged. Then she got up and started dancing along behind her grandmother.

They went around the sofa, and over to the window, and back.

"Up and at 'em, Pete," said Mrs. Bowditch over her shoulder.

"I don't want to break *my* hip!" I said.

"Come *on!*" said Rootie.

I got up and joined the line.

One-two-three—kick!

I was beginning to get into it. "Serpentine, Rootie," I said. "Serpentine!"

"Where are you going after your reunion?" called Rootie.

"A friend has offered to lend me her house in Saratoga for August," said Mrs. Bowditch. "I thought we might watch some races."

Saratoga. I couldn't believe it.

"That would be cool," said Rootie. "Could we take Mooshy along?"

"Certainly," said Mrs. Bowditch.

"And Franklin?" said Rootie.

"Absolutely," said Mrs. Bowditch.

Oklahoma.

Maybe Biscuit was still there.

"How about you, Pete?" said Mrs. Bowditch. "Want to come along?"

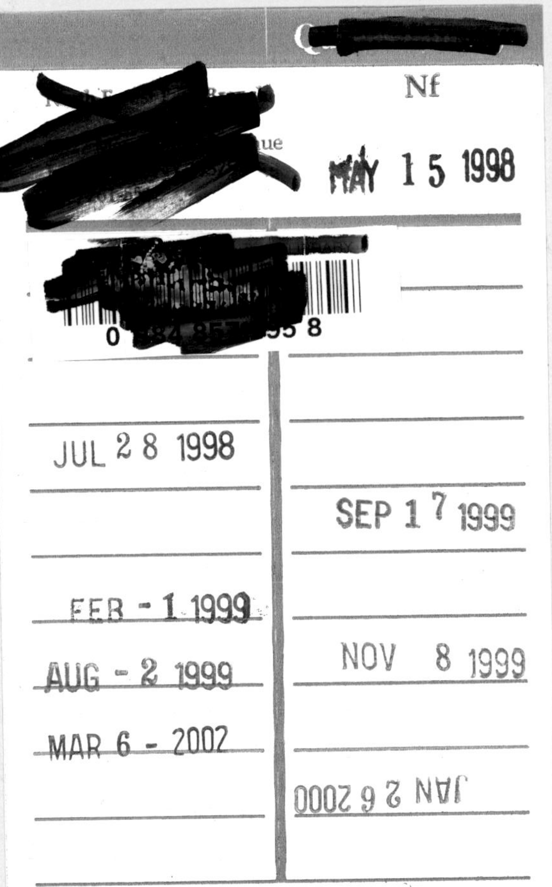
Nf
MAY 15 1998
JUL 28 1998
SEP 17 1999
FEB - 1 1999
AUG - 2 1999
NOV 8 1999
MAR 6 - 2002
All items are due on latest date stamped. A charge is made for each day, including Sundays and holidays, that this item is overdue.
420-1-8/91

LIBRARY